JUNE FOSTER

What God Knew

By June Foster

Copyright © 2019 by June Foster
Published by Forget Me Not Romances

This book is a work of fiction. Names, characters, places, and incidents are the product of the author's imagination and are used fictitiously. Any resemblance to actual events, locales, or persons, living or dead, is coincidental.

All rights reserved including the right to reproduce this book or portions thereof in any form whatsoever – except short passages for reviews – without express permission.

ISBN-13: 979-8-8691-3716-6

Copyright 2019 by June Foster
Published by Forget Me Not Romances

This book is a work of fiction. Names, characters, places, and incidents are the product of the author's imagination and are used fictitiously. Any resemblance to actual events, locales, or persons, living or dead, is coincidental.

All rights reserved including the right to reproduce this book or portions thereof in any form whatsoever – except short passages for reviews – without express permission.

Chapter One

Michael straightened the name tag on his lab jacket identifying him as a neonatal team member at El Camino General and tapped on the hospital room door. He opened his mouth to announce his presence but snapped it shut. Dave Reyes, father of the preemie baby girl, bent over his wife's bed. Closed eyes and clasped hands relayed the message. The couple was praying.

Only one thing to do. Stand quietly inside the threshold and wait. Prayer. We needed more of that.

"And, Lord, we ask you to allow little Abby to develop and grow strong. We know You cherish this new life, and we offer her up to You. Even her name means Joy to the Father. Her mother and I pray that our daughter will bring You joy all the days of her life. In Jesus' Name."

Mrs. Reyes opened tear-filled eyes and whisked the moisture from her cheek.

"Good morning, Mr. and Mrs. Reyes." Michael stepped closer to the bed. "How are you today?" He trained his gaze on the pretty blonde still clutching the hand of her dark-haired husband.

"We're doing well, thank you. And please call us Betty Ann and Dave," Mrs. Reyes said.

Dave left his wife's side and walked toward Michael with an extended hand. "Thanks for coming in, Dr. Clark. We're both anxious to hear about our daughter."

Though Michael had treated cases of preemies who were born as early as twenty-six weeks, little Abby stood a better chance of survival at thirty-two weeks. "Your baby has indications of jaundice, but we're treating her with phototherapy. She'll be fed with a feeding tube for a while, but I'd encourage you to supply breast milk if you're planning to nurse her."

Betty Ann nodded. "Yes, I definitely want to provide her milk."

"Excellent. At present we're keeping her in an incubator. The good news is there are no signs of apnea and bradycardia. I anticipate you'll be able to take her home in about four weeks." Though Michael felt confident that this child would thrive, he never viewed any case as routine. Every child was unique, God's precious gift to parents.

"Thank you, Lord." Dave glanced at the ceiling and back to Michael.

"Dr. Clark, when will we be able to see her?" Betty Ann wiped another tear from her eye.

Michael smiled. "As soon as you feel up to making the trip to the NIC unit. I'm sure you'll be encouraged by our caring staff."

Betty Ann turned to Dave and squeezed his arm. "I'd like to go this afternoon."

Casting a loving glance at his wife, Dave patted her hand. "We'll go over there together." He looked up to Michael. "Doctor, we've placed our baby in God's hands, and we're praying for you and the entire staff in the NIC unit."

"That's the best thing you can do." Dave sounded like Michael's mother, telling others how prayer works. Since early childhood, he'd listened to her Bible stories and constant prayers. Though, as a doctor, he trusted in science and modern medicine, Michael believed God's power transcended any healing a medical professional might offer. "Well, nice chatting with you both." He handed his card to Dave. "Here's my private cell number if you need to call me. Please feel free."

"Thank you, Doctor. We appreciate your availability and medical care for our baby girl." Dave cleared his throat, as if stifling an emotion.

"You're welcome." Michael gripped Abby Reyes' records in his hand and walked out the door and into the hall. He blinked his eyes, relishing the image of Dave and Betty Ann Reyes talking to God. A rare sight in the hospital as too many people ignored Him these days.

*****

Tammy Crawford bent over the elderly man not wanting to believe the signs of eminent death: thinning of the skin and a pale face. His eyes fluttered open a moment, and the corners of his mouth lifted in a weak smile.

"Hello, Pumpkin." He coughed in an attempt to catch his breath.

She sat in the bedside chair and grasped his hand, already showing the bluish color of cyanosis caused by low oxygen saturation. "You know, my grandpa used to call me that. He said my red hair reminded him of a Halloween pumpkin." She attempted a smile in return.

Wrinkles etched lines on his kindly face, and liver spots dotted his skin. White hair protruded in disheveled clumps.

At the head of the bed, the EKG machine beeped, indicating a change in blood pressure. Tammy glanced at the reading. Sixty-eight over forty-five. No doubt the inevitable would happen. Probably within moments. Mr. Gruening's ischemic heart disease, complicated by hypertension, contributed to his condition, but she didn't want him to die.

He squeezed her hand. "Pumpkin, the Lord is calling me home pretty soon. An angel's coming to take me to Jesus."

Dread and fear filled Tammy. Sure she'd seen other patients die, but this was somehow different. "Please, sir, just hang on." She swallowed the threatening tears. "You can make it."

He closed his eyes and opened them again. "Jesus is waiting for me in my eternal home."

Mr. Gruening's thoughts of a better place were nice for those nearing the end. She didn't want to take that away from him in his final moments. Too bad there was no truth in them. She needed to be practical. Bodies only decayed after a person died.

The patient coughed, his breathing patterns erratic. With one last breath, he let out a long sigh and closed his eyelids.

Tammy glanced at the monitor once again. The machine flat lined. Mr. Gruening had slipped away. Dampness trailed to her chin before she even realized a tear had released. The most difficult part of her job as a geriatrics nurse was death. A slight smile sat on his face, which displayed a look of utter peace. She pulled the sheet over his head and whispered. "Good-bye, sir. I truly hope you are with Jesus." If only that were true. Rising from her seat by the side of his bed, she gulped down the tears. The memory of her grandfather's death years ago stabbed her heart once again—her grandpa, the only person who loved Tammy for who she was, not always trying to change her like her sister and parents.

Stifling the heartache, she took his chart and noted the exact time of his passing. Then she left the room. The next step—contacting the geriatrics doctor on duty to verify the death.

*****

Tammy pushed open the glass door of the main doctor's lounge angry with herself for allowing the unprofessional emotion to escape. At least she hadn't let her feelings show when the attending doctor examined the patient and confirmed the time of death on the chart. To do so would expose vulnerability. She couldn't permit him to perceive her as incompetent. The only way to prove her self-worth was through hard work and excellence in performance.

Gripping her fists into tight balls, she headed toward the counter where the coffee pot sat. If Mr. Gruening had taken better care of himself, maybe he'd still be alive. If only he'd adhered to proper diet and exercise. If he'd learned at an early age that overeating and a sedentary lifestyle greatly affected his physical condition, then he wouldn't have had as many medical problems.

The paper cups from the cabinet would do. She reached for one as the same pesky heaviness she'd endured at Grandpa's funeral, invaded her. Gritting her teeth, she poured the hot liquid.

Once again she looked away, trying to push the pain of loss from her. Heat swarmed over her hand that held the cup in place. She yelped, nearly dropping the pot. Setting it on the counter, she grabbed a paper towel, wiped her hand and mopped up spilled coffee.

"May I do that for you?" A smooth masculine voice offered.

When she turned around, a doctor whose warm, brown

complexion matched the richness of his tone stood in front of her. "Thanks."

He laughed. "I guess the only bright spot about burning your hand is you're in a hospital with plenty of doctors." He filled her cup with hot coffee, steam rising from the liquid. "Would you like cream?"

"No, thanks." Tammy took in the name on his ID tag: Dr. Michael Clark, Neonatal Pediatrician. "It's never easy to lose someone I've cared for on the floor, but a dear man, one of my favorite patients, just died."

"Sit down a minute and join me while you drink your coffee." He pointed to the comfortable couch along the wall. "I think that's one of the toughest things required of medical personnel. We're expected to be objective about every case, but it's hard to ignore our own human emotions. Whether a preemie or an elderly person, it never gets easier." His gaze dropped to her nametag. "Tammy Crawford. I'm Michael Clark."

Tammy sank down on the leather couch and took a sip of the hot liquid, careful not to spill it. Letting out a long breath, she allowed her gaze to take in the man she'd found so handsome. Long lashes surrounded deep brown eyes. His dark hair was cut short to his head. Closely shaven cheeks and skin the color of a caramel latte intrigued her. "So you're in the neonatal unit."

"Yeah, I'm one of several on the team. We have a professional and efficient group of nurse practitioners, RN's, and doctors." He tilted his head as his gaze fixed on her. "Are you feeling better?"

His compassion made her want to shed tears again. "Yeah, thanks. One thing that didn't help. The patient reminded me of my grandfather. I lost him when I was ten, and then my mom died last year." She gave herself a mental kick. Why was she telling this man her life story, something she usually didn't do?

Michael frowned. "That's hard. I'm sorry. When I lose a baby, at least I have the assurance that he or she is with the Lord."

Some people believed that one goes to live with God when they die. But she'd never been able to embrace the stories from the Bible she'd learned in Sunday school as a child.

Once again, Dr. Clark's comforting smile almost evoked the emotion she'd held at bay. If she hung around any longer, she might be consumed by troublesome tears. She stood and tossed her paper coffee cup in the garbage. "Guess I better go. Nice to meet you, Michael."

He gazed at her with dreamy brown eyes and smiled. "Same here, Tammy."

As she headed out the door, Mr. Gruening's words bore into her heart, and she couldn't erase the image of his face from her thoughts. "I'm going home."

Where was Mr. Gruening right now? Had he merely ceased to exist or had he passed on to the same place Michael said his babies go?

Chapter Two

Michael parked his Mercedes in front of the sprawling gray brick home. Dad must've hired a yard man. The shrubs were neatly trimmed, and fall leaves were raked up into a neat pile. The lush lawn surrounding the house had begun to turn brown with the cooler days of November in El Camino, California. He pushed through the unlocked door into the entryway, the aroma of some kind of roasted meat tickling his nose and making his stomach growl. The expansive living room with the stone fireplace lay straight ahead.

"Hello. I'm not late for dinner, am I?" He chuckled. An invitation to eat a home-cooked meal at Mom and Dad's was always welcome since he wasn't much of a cook. Too, this last week had kept him busy with little time for more than frozen dinners every night.

His mom, her chestnut eyes shining, walked into the hall from the kitchen, wiping her hands on her apron. She tiptoed and planted a kiss on his cheek. "You're right on time. Darnell just arrived a few moments ago. He's in the living room with Dad. We got back from church an hour ago, but I had everything already prepared."

Dad, a church goer? "Since when did he start going to services? He used not to find the time."

"Your father has attended with me for a couple of months now. As you know, your sister and I have been praying for him." She gave Michael a hug. "I praise God for two of my kids who're walking with the Lord," she whispered. "Now we've got to pray for Darnell a little harder."

"Yep. Maybe I could get him to come with me sometime." Though Michael attended a church near the airport, he wasn't as active as he'd like to be since his medical practice took so much of his time.

A contagious grin filled Mom's face, evoking Michael's smile. "You know, Alexus and the boys will be out for a visit in a couple of weeks. Make sure you reserve an evening. Dad and I would like to have a family dinner."

"Sounds great, Mom. Her husband isn't coming?"

"No. The architectural firm is keeping him busy. But I can't wait to see my grandsons." She fisted his shoulder. "But back to you. How are things in your life? Anybody interesting you haven't told me about?"

"Mom, you know I don't have time to date right now." He circled his arm around her shoulders and gave her a kiss on the cheek. "Let's go in the living room so I can say hi to Dad and Darnell." Even if he was dating someone, he'd try to keep the details from Mom. She'd switch the subject to marriage and grandbabies before he could utter another word.

Dad reclined in the overstuffed easy chair, sipping a cup of coffee. He glanced up and motioned to Michael to sit down. "Hey, son. How's the doctor business?"

"Good to see you, bro." Darnell stood and slapped him on the back.

Mom called from the dining room. "Don't get too comfortable in there, boys. Dinner's on the table."

The dining room off the living room accommodated the massive mahogany table, minus one leaf today, a china cabinet, side buffet, and Mom's paintings she'd created from areas where they'd lived all over Europe when Michael was a child. Life as an army general's son had been an adventure, adapting to the various cultures of Dad's duty stations.

"Sit in your usual places. Michael, across from Darnell and Dad and I at either end," Mom said.

Michael edged down into the upholstered chair and placed the linen napkin in his lap. Mom had a flair for decor and setting an elegant table.

"Willie, can you please say grace?"

Dad saying grace? Amazing. Something that didn't happen when Michael was a child. But then Dad always seemed to be deployed or at a high-level army conference.

Clearing his deep baritone voice, his father folded his hands. "Lord, we're truly grateful for this meal my sweet wife, Chelsea, has prepared. Please bless it to our nourishment. Amen."

Michael lifted his head and opened his eyes. Darnell peered over Michael's shoulder at the light green wall. Had he remained like that during the entire prayer?

Bowls filled with green beans, buttery corn-on-the-cob, thick beef stew, and a mixed salad filled the table. "Boys, how about some homemade hot rolls?" Mom handed a basket to him.

"Now, Chelsea, they're not boys any more. They're two grown men with outstanding careers. I'm proud of both of you." He turned to Darnell. "Your organization does a lot to help the less fortunate in our area. What's your latest project?"

Darnell swallowed a bite of stew. "I'm in the process of identifying affordable housing available in the Pacific Northwest, as far as Seattle, and placing qualifying clients in their new homes."

"The need reminds me so much of the days when your father was stationed at Ft. Gordon in Georgia." Mom passed the stew around the table. "My, that area had their share of poverty stricken neighborhoods."

Memories flooded back to Michael. "It was because you used to haul me around on your ministry trips to those neighborhoods that I decided to become a pediatrician."

Mom smiled. "God had His plan. I remember that day we visited one apartment house. Lillie May, the other lady from church, came with us. We packed a lunch in a basket and tossed in a Bible and a couple of tracts. I gathered you up and off we went."

"I was in school in those days and didn't go with you and Michael. But I suppose even then you influenced me to reach out to needy families." Darnell lifted a brow. "Since childhood, I've wanted our people to break free of the ghettos and poverty that limits them."

"And I've always admired that in you, Darnell. I suppose I went down to those neighborhoods because I wanted to make time for the most important things—serving God and reaching out to those that hadn't heard the gospel."

Michael swallowed a bite of green beans. "That was the day I knew I wanted to be a doctor. Seeing a little boy with the coughing fits did something to me." He gazed at his family with a smile. "I knew I had to dedicate my life to helping children like him. Today croup can be treated. It's no longer a threat."

"There were a few times I worried about you two." Dad sipped his iced tea. "Gallivanting around in those neighborhoods of Augusta."

"What bothered me the most were the young women fraternizing with the soldiers at Ft. Gordon, many getting pregnant and the young men leaving them behind." Mom frowned. "A particular girl really got to me, the one with that pretty brown baby with blue eyes. She didn't know what to do, getting pregnant and being shunned by the boy's parents. They wanted nothing to do with a mixed-race baby."

"And you would be more accepting, Mom? If I recall, you were still holding on to the old way of thinking, too. Mixed racial marriages are not an anomaly these days." Michael said.

Mom chewed a bite of bread and swallowed. "I suppose what worries me the most are those girls, any girls raising children on their own. It shouldn't be."

"But then we have agencies like Darnell's to assist." Dad wiped his mouth with his napkin.

"That's not the point. Mom's right. White dudes come on to the black girls until they get what they want, and then they walk away. Or white girls … they hang on to the black guys who have clout. Black people need to have enough pride to stay away from that kind of manipulation." Darnell raised his voice to a questionable level. "Some things never change. When a black person hooks up with a white, they're fraternizing with their worst enemy, and they don't even have an idea about it until whitey's done dropped a bomb on them."

Dad frowned. "Darnell, I've seen the enemy on the battlefield. This is America, not Vietnam. We are not at war with each other here."

"In some neighborhoods, people with brown skin are still crossing some invisible line and getting stopped and frisked for no reason. Heck, in college I got pulled over in a white subdivision because I was driving Dad's Lincoln—like the cop thought I'd stolen it." Darnell blew out a frustrated sigh and glared at Michael. "They stopped me because I fit a profile?" He ran his fingers along his arm. "No, my skin tone alone tells whitey I'm untrustworthy." Darnell dropped his fork with a clink. "Now tell me. Would anyone want to connect with a race that's responsible for those kinds of injustices?"

"Honey, you never told me you feel like that, but in your heart you know you weren't driving a stolen car. You're accountable to God not men. And you're painting a very wide brush with those strokes. The white people aren't our enemy, and the anger I hear in your voice. It makes me shudder. You shouldn't hold it in your heart like that," Mom said.

Dad turned to Michael and cleared his throat. "Son, what are your immediate goals these days? You're doing well. Maybe it's time for you to settle down."

"Go ahead. Change the subject." Darnell scoffed and rolled his eyes.

Michael was caught between two competing entities: his brother's prejudice and his parents' passive aggressive stance on issues. He forced away the rebellion he might have displayed in the past. "No time for that right now. I'd like to work on bringing a specialty pediatrics hospital that includes a topnotch neonatal unit to El Camino."

"What?" Darnell laughed. "You're going to give up the big bucks, bro?"

"Now, Darnell." Mom patted his hand. "We can't discount the possibility that God has placed a very worthy desire in Michael's heart."

"Mom, get real." Darnell shook his head. "God doesn't just reach down from Heaven and deposit a notion in somebody's head. I run a non-profit. How do you think I make things work? Through hard work, determination, and donations from people and institutions."

Michael lifted his gaze to his brother's scowling face. Was Michael foolish for going that route? Or had God placed the desire there, like Mom said?

*****

Two days later, Michael still pondered his brother's comments about God. Despite Darnell's objections, his mother had been right. God gave him the burden to build a specialty children's hospital in El Camino. He held his head a bit higher as he walked from his office on the pediatric floor and down the hall to the NIC unit. If anyone could bring this to pass, it had to be him.

His colleague and close friend, Dr. Jeff Valentine, bent over one of the incubators along the wall, listening to a baby's heartbeat with his stethoscope. He glanced up as Michael approached. "Hey, Michael. I was getting ready to take off. Hope you have a good rest of the day." He marked the infant's chart and ambled toward his office in the hall near Michael's.

"Yeah, thanks." Michael patted Jeff's shoulder as he passed. "See you tomorrow." Nearing the middle of the room, he paused at the Reyes' baby's crib. The preemie fed by mouth now, breathed on her own, and the jaundice was replaced by pink, healthy-looking skin.

As soon as Dave and Betty Ann arrived for their daily visit, he'd give them the good news. Based on little Abby weight, she might go home a couple of weeks earlier than he thought. He glanced at her chart to check the last several entries. NP Jerry Taylor's submissions were detailed, avoiding the common charting mistakes such as failing to report every nursing action performed or medications administered. Neatly written notes filled the pages, each recording the baby's heart rate, breathing rate, and oxygen saturation.

"Hello, Dr. Clark." Betty Ann Reyes' bright blue eyes glistened as she and Dave walked toward the incubator.

"Just the two people I wanted to see. I've got great news. Your baby is stable, and you should be able to take her home in two more weeks."

Moisture glistened in Betty Ann's eyes as she gripped Dave's hands. "Oh, thank you, Doctor. That's an answer to prayer. Her big sister, Alice, can't wait to have her at home."

Dave stepped forward and shook Michael's hand. "Thank you, Dr. Clark. We're planning Abby's baby dedication in about a month. We'd love for you to come."

"I'd be honored. Let me know when." Michael enjoyed getting involved with his patients' families.

The buzz of his beeper sounded the dreaded alarm. He glanced at the typed message. A baby was in distress—the Sanchez' infant.

He raced toward the child's crib, glancing over his shoulder at the Reyes parents. "Excuse me."

NP Taylor leaned over the incubator and attempted resuscitation.

Stepping in front of her, he continued her efforts, dread gripping him. Losing a baby was an area of his job he'd never been able to reconcile. After ten minutes, he finally stopped when he saw no change in the Cardiopulmonary Monitor.

He turned to Mrs. Taylor standing by his side and shook his head. "I'm so sorry, Jerry."

Moisture gathered in her eyes. "Doctor, he had been stable only an hour ago. I can't understand it. Everything was going so well. The labs indicated no problems." She gulped. "I'd even taught the parents how to feed their little guy. We neglected nothing. Every shift nurse worked hard. Even Dr. Valentine thought the baby was doing well. I'd only left his side for a minute, and when I came back, he'd stopped breathing."

Pain gripped Michael's heart like it must've ripped through Jerry's now. She was a capable nurse practitioner, and he knew she grieved as he did. "I guarantee that this is not your fault. I have the greatest respect for your work."

Jerry rested a hand on her chest. "Thank you, Dr. Clark, for your assurance. That means so much to me. But I hate more than anything telling the parents."

"I'll do it. Don't worry." He squeezed her shoulder.

Jerry dabbed a tissue to her eyes. "I'm grateful."

The baby's chart contained to the parents' contact information. Though Jerry hurt, he determined to maintain his doctor persona, masking his emotions at the loss of this child. It would difficult enough for the mother and father.

He'd wait in the NIC unit until the they arrived. Now, more than ever, he realized the need for a specialty hospital. He could bring in the most qualified doctors in the US. Extra corporeal membrane oxygenation was a life-saving treatment for newborns with severe breathing difficulties. If he'd been able to provide

ECMO, the baby might have survived. If only one child's life could be saved, the cost of opening a specialty hospital would be worth every penny.

WHAT GOD KNEW

Chapter Three

Tammy set the patient's chart on the counter above her workspace. Her phone rang. Joella. "Hello, sis."

"Hey, girl. I'm on my way to the NIC unit to meet Betty Ann and Dave and visit Baby Abby. Dr. Clark told them they could take Abby home in a few weeks, and they're so excited. You want to come, too? Do you have a break anytime soon?"

Tammy glanced at the wall clock. "Sure, I haven't taken my lunch hour yet. This would be a good time. I'll meet you on the pediatrics floor." Besides a visit with Joella, there'd be another advantage of going up to the neonatal clinic. She might run into the hunky doctor she'd met in the lounge.

"Great. I'll be there in thirty minutes."

Babies, babies. Was that all her sister could think of? Tammy had other things to contemplate in her life, like her career. "See you in a bit."

By the time Tammy had finished her current stack of paper work, a half hour had escaped. She turned to her colleague working on the other side. "Mildred, if you don't mind, I'm going to take my lunch now."

She gave Tammy a nod. "Sure. See you later."

Tammy took the elevator up to the seventh floor and stepped out into the short hall that led to the NIC unit.

Farther down, Joella leaned against the counter at the nurses' station chatting with the woman on duty, Tammy's friend from nursing school, Charlotte Sperry.

"Hi, Charlotte." Tammy smiled at her peer then turned toward Joella. "Hey, Sis. How's baby Jacob?"

Joella's eyes lit with happiness. "He took his first steps the other night. You should've seen JD's face. He literally beamed with pride. I still can't get it through my skull. Our son will be one this month." Then a furrow creased her brow, and she studied her clasped hands. "It's hard to comprehend that Mom never really got to know her grandson. He was only four months old when she died."

Mom's death had impacted Tammy, too, in so many ways. If the day came when she had children, Mom wouldn't be there to see any of them grow up. "It's still a shock to me. Her cancer spread so quickly. But why do you think Dad sold the house and took off to Europe?"

Joella looked at the tiled floor. "I suppose he needed to leave the area that held so many memories. I think Mom's passing did something to him—deep inside."

"I'm sure you're right." Tammy nodded. "I don't think he's open to communicating with us right now."

"I hate to admit it, but I agree. He left in such a rush, he didn't even give us a forwarding address. All I have is a cell phone number—if it still works. I'm not sure what's going on in his mind. He'll return to our lives someday when the time is right."

"Hey, do you remember Mom telling us about the long walks they took by the bubbling waters, as she used to describe it, of Big Lunas Creek in lower Osmond Park?"

Joella's gazed off somewhere over Tammy's shoulder. "That place holds significance for me and JD as well. We had our first kiss there."

Sentimentality like Joella's seemed foreign to Tammy. She only understood the difficulties of relationships. "I just feel so empty without Dad. The thought that I can't run to my daddy like I did when I was a kid hurts. The man whose strong arms used to protect and comfort me is in a different continent now."

"I do recall you two had your differences," Joella said.

"I know. I always thought he was too strict, but I'd love some of that guidance now." Tammy sighed then looked up at the smiling couple with the little girl in tow, stepping off the elevator and heading toward them.

Betty Ann Reyes, as slender as before the baby's birth, grinned. "Little Abby is going home soon. Can you believe it?"

"Knowing you, Betty Ann, your nursery looks like a picture out of a Babies "R" Us catalogue." Joella smiled.

Betty Ann laughed. "You probably remember when I decorated Alice's bedroom soon after she arrived at Dave's home."

"I still remember, Mommy." The smiling child grinned up at Betty Ann.

Dave's wife looked down at the girl. "That's right, honey." She glanced up again at Joella. "Wow, it's been almost two years." She gave Dave an adoring look.

"Abby will have her own space in the former guest room, but she'll be with us for a while in her bassinette," Dave said. "Honestly, if the Lord sends us another baby, the new one will have to bunk with Abby—or else the church will need to move us to a larger house. And to think I used to rattle around in there thinking it was too big."

"No more babies for a while, my dear husband." Betty Ann poked him in the ribs.

Joella lifted her gaze to a person walking toward them from the interior of the unit and her face brightened.

An attractive young woman with a long brown ponytail flitted up to them.

"Hey, Glorilyn. What are you doing here?" Joella said.

"I'm a volunteer with the NICU Cuddling Program and took advantage of my afternoon off." Glorilyn grinned. "My kindergarteners only came to school for a half day today." She glanced at Dave and Betty Ann. "I had the privilege of rocking your little one last week."

Betty Ann laughed. "She's going to be spoiled before we even get her home."

"You remember my sister, Tammy," Joella said. "Tammy, this is Glorilyn Neilson, JD's sister."

"Yes, hi. I don't think I've seen you since Joella's baby shower, though," Glorilyn said.

Tammy tossed a strand of hair behind her ear. "That has been a while."

"Well, nice seeing all of you." Dave grasped his daughter's hand and looked at his wife. "Ready, you two? Let's go visit with

Abby."

"I believe NICU only allows two visitors accompanied by the parents, not counting big sisters, of course." Tammy glanced at Joella. "We'd better tag along with Betty Ann and Dave. Oh, yes, and we need to sterilize our hands over there." She pointed to the sink near the nurses' station and waved at Joella's sister-in-law. "Take care, Glorilyn."

"Bye, everybody. I need to go home and make lesson plans for tomorrow." Glorilyn hugged both Joella and Tammy and turned toward the entrance.

After they all washed their hands, Alice dashed toward Abby's crib. She stood on tiptoe and sang "Rock-A-Bye Baby" to the child.

The scene struck a chord deep inside. Would Tammy ever experience a tender moment like that if she had children?

She trailed behind the others, still filled with awe. Glancing to her right, she saw Michael Clark a few spaces over examining an infant. With graceful movements, he slid his stethoscope around on the baby's chest. Then he carefully moved the child to its side, Michael's hand larger than the baby's head. He looked into the left ear with his otoscope as the infant sucked on a pacifier that reached from ear to ear. The compassion Michael wore on his caramel-brown face warmed Tammy's heart. He'd committed himself to the well-being of his tiny patients. Something important to her as well. An inner smile dawned inside.

At Abby's crib, Betty Ann leaned over her sleeping daughter, whose little legs were drawn up under her tummy. "Hello, little angel," Betty Ann cooed.

"God has greatly blessed us." Dave grinned. "He's allowed our little girl to thrive and provided an excellent doctor. I can't say enough good about Dr. Clark."

Tammy looked from the Reyes child back to Michael still hovering over the same baby. Her gaze slid to his ring finger on his left hand. No circle of gold. The lack of a wedding band didn't say much though. A lot of guys didn't wear them. She'd have to confirm his marital status with Charlotte.

The more she thought about him, the more the idea of becoming better acquainted appealed to her. Though she'd always considered herself a career woman, nothing stood in her way of having a captivating boyfriend. If she were honest, between his thoughtful actions the other day and his obvious professional dedication to his little patients, he'd risen to the top of her "Mr. Perfect" list.

After several more minutes, Joella turned to her. "Well, I guess I'd better leave for home. Baby Jacob's with a sitter, and JD's coming home early today." She laughed. "Jacob looks like a giant compared to Abby."

"There's almost a year between the two, you know." Tammy glanced at her watch. "I've got to return to work as well." She looked toward the Reyes couple. "Congratulations on your new baby."

Both Dave and Betty Ann glanced at her with a grin and then back to their infant.

When Tammy followed Joella out of the NIC unit, she gazed one last time at Michael Clark. She'd have to figure out a way to become better acquainted with the good looking pediatrician—if he wasn't married.

As they stepped into the elevator, Joella peered at her. "So, Tammy, how are your nursing applications coming along? I haven't heard you talking about anything else, well since you broke up with Ted."

Ted, that bum. So irresponsible. Nothing like Dr. Clark. She shook her head. No, she wouldn't share her interest in the alluring doctor—not now. "I'm planning on becoming qualified as a nurse practitioner and taking courses on line."

"Hey, I'm really proud of you little sister." Joella beamed.

"Thanks." Becoming a nurse practitioner insured job security and higher pay but more importantly, she'd bring expert help to her patients, similar to the care Dr. Clark gave to his preemies. She pressed the button for the lobby. "You married a good husband, but you still have the ability to take care of yourself and Jacob with your training as an interior designer. That's what I have to do. I never want to be in a position where I have to depend on a man."

*****

Tammy stood in the hospital lobby peering out at the stormy afternoon. Raindrops the size of small pebbles splattered the sidewalk and parking lot. A flash of lightning split the darkened sky and thunder echoed, sounding like a giant grumbling ogre.

She zipped up her jacket and pushed the button to open her umbrella. The lever wouldn't budge. She poked again. Nothing. The old contraption needed to find a home in the garbage can.

Gripping the useless thing in one hand, she hoisted her purse on her shoulder and pushed through the glass doors. She'd have to forge on despite the weather. A little rain never hurt anybody.

With careful steps, she maneuvered the wet sidewalks. The rain soaking through her clothes, she increased her pace to her car at the end of the second row. She dared to take quicker steps and focused on the ground, heading straight ahead.

A pair of feet appeared in front of her before she could stop the momentum. *Bam. Whoosh.* A person landed on the pavement.

Tammy gasped. Michael Clark lay prone on the ground clutching his chest, his white lab jacket a muddy mess. The sharp end of her wayward umbrella had somehow knocked him backwards, and he'd slipped in a puddle of water. "Oh, Doctor." She dropped her umbrella and reached to help him up.

"It's Michael." Holding on with one hand and pushing up with the other, he rose to his feet. "Remind me not to tangle with you again—or your vicious umbrella the next time I'm not paying attention." He smirked.

The rain continued to pelt her scrubs, soaking all the way to her skin, but looking up at him, a rush of pleasure warmed her. "Are you okay?"

Still rubbing his chest, he opened up his umbrella and held it over her. "Oh, sure. Just a stab wound to the solar plexus, but I'll get over it."

Despite the serious potential of their accident, she laughed. "I didn't realize how lethal an umbrella is. I'm so sorry."

He winked. "No harm done. Don't think I need first aid."

Tammy grinned, drops of water dripping from her hair. "All right then." She picked up her useless umbrellas and started to move on.

"Let me walk you to your car, Nurse Crawford."

She nodded, savoring his nearness next to her. The smell of rain and his aftershave were intoxicating.

When she pressed the unlock button, Michael reached his

broad forearm across in front of her and held the door open. "Try not to stab anyone else. They may not be as resilient."

She laughed. "What were you thinking about? I mean what kept you from paying attention?" She lowered into the driver's seat.

"Just a project I'm working on, but maybe in the future I should concentrate more on attractive nurses wielding dangerous weapons. Have a nice evening, Nurse Tammy."

She smiled at him and started the engine.

Michael nodded and turned back to the hospital.

Her grin felt as if it reached all the way across her lips. The good looking doctor had flirted with her.

Chapter Four

The next day, Tammy studied the diagnostic reports she'd just received but thoughts of Michael lingered. She shook her head and tried to focus on finding Mr. Hagel's ID and lab results on the computer.

The phone rang, and she reached for it. "Geriatrics floor, Tammy Crawford."

"Tammy, this is Mildred." The voice on the other end was clearly rattled.

"Hi, Mildred. Are you enjoying your week off from work?"

She sighed. "I will as of tomorrow. We're leaving and taking the kids to Disneyland. But I have to finish up some incident reports then pack for all four of them. I need to ask you a huge favor."

"Sure. What is it?"

"On your way home tonight, could you drop by my house and pick up the reports? I'm snowed under trying to get my husband and these kids ready to go plus finish up these records for the hospital."

Since she didn't have anywhere she needed to be after work, she'd have plenty of time. "Sure. Give me your address."

Mildred repeated the house numbers and street, and Tammy jotted it down.

"I can't thank you enough."

"No problem. See you later." She hung up the phone and glanced back at the computer screen, recording Mr. Hagel's information on his chart.

After several minutes, she looked up. The nurse in charge of the department approached with a smile and gripped a fistful of tickets in her hand.

"Tammy, El Camino Hospital Auxiliary Society is sponsoring a charity banquet. And you'll never guess what else. You remember Mr. Gruening?"

Tammy raised a brow. Why would her boss be so excited about a patient who'd passed away? "Yes. Clyde Gruening."

"Well, his daughter is head of the society and was so grateful for the excellent care her father received before he died that she intends to give special recognition to our department, which includes a monetary donation at the banquet ceremony. As I understand it, other departments will benefit, too, but the geriatrics will receive the largest donation."

Tammy plopped back in her chair. "That's wonderful."

"As many employees as possible from our unit are encouraged to attend as well as help sell tickets." She thrust a packet into Tammy's hand. "Here are some. I've got more if you sell these. The banquet is in a month. "

"I'd be happy to." Having her department cited in a positive way was exciting. Hopefully, Mr. Reynolds, the hospital administrator, would get the word as well. So many times, hospital units were written up for negligence and issued warnings. Nice to do something right for a change. "I'm going to talk to a few more people on our floor."

Tammy walked toward the doctor's lounge clutching the brightly colored vouchers. She could call Joella to see if she and JD would be interested. Her sister could definitely afford it.

Then a different thought inched into her mind. What if she made another trip to the NIC unit to see if Charlotte would be interested in a ticket but just happened to run into Dr. Clark's office to sell him one? She checked the clock on the wall. Time for a quick break.

On her way up, she'd call Joella to see if she wanted to meet for lunch. Maybe even enlist her to sell a few tickets.

*****

Michael circled his office desk, his cell phone plastered to his ear. "Yes, I spoke with my business consultant, and he sounded positive about the venture. I appreciate your interest, Mr. Jamison. I'll talk to you soon." Michael punched *off* and dropped the phone back in his pocket. The wealthy entrepreneur sounded receptive to financing Michael's project and would clear his schedule for their meeting in the next couple of days. Drawing his elbow down, he fisted his hand in the victory motion.

The first two hurdles in realizing his dream of a specialty hospital in El Camino seemed to fall into place. Michael lifted his gaze to the ceiling. A business plan and now an investor. If Mr. Jamison's offer was substantial enough, Michael might only need one financier. Now the next step was to gather a group of people willing to serve as board of directors.

Though it might be too early to celebrate the success of the new hospital, exhilaration circled around him like a dive into icy water. The plan seemed to be falling into place. What could possibly go wrong?

Reaching down to the desk top, he closed the file where he kept the paper work and other documents for the new hospital. Time to make his rounds. He strolled out to the main office.

Iris Canton, his elderly but loveable secretary, pushed reading glasses up on her nose and squinted at her computer. Though he'd found more than one mistake lately, he couldn't bear to recommend she retire or report her to Mr. Reynolds. The several times she'd talked about her personal life, she'd always spoken of her grandson whom she was putting through college. Iris, no doubt, needed this job. Besides, he couldn't get along without her kindly smile every morning.

She looked up as he neared her desk. "Dr. Clark, how are you today? You know, I was bragging on you to my grandson. I told him what a fine doctor you were and how you worked hard to get through medical school. Told him never give up. Determination always pays off in the end."

Sure he'd persevered in school, but now he'd reached one of his goals, becoming a qualified, skillful pediatrician. And he was proud of it. "Keep on reminding him. It never hurts. Right now I'm using some of that determination to make the specialty hospital I told you about the other day a reality. I'll do anything to see it come about. I'm telling you, Iris, if I have to sell my townhouse and move in with my family, I will."

"Oh, Dr. Clark, are you moving—"

Michael's pager beeped and he glanced at the message. *You're needed immediately on the NIC unit.*

Must be an emergency. "Excuse me, Iris."

*****

Tammy stepped out of the elevator on the seventh floor, bypassing the NICU. She took the hall that led to Michael's office and walked through the double doors.

An elderly woman with short, curly white hair, tapped on the keys of her computer. She looked up with a pleasant smile. "Yes, what can I do for you?"

"Hi, I'm Tammy Crawford from the geriatrics floor." Tammy stuck out her hand. "The El Camino Hospital Auxiliary is having a benefit for the hospital, and I thought perhaps Dr. Clark might be interested in purchasing tickets since the NIC unit will receive part of the proceeds." The statement wasn't dishonest as the entire hospital would profit from the income.

The name plaque on her desk said *Iris Canton*. Iris shook her head, tight white curls bouncing. "I'm afraid the Clarks won't be in town. I just got the news today. He's selling his townhouse and moving his family from El Camino." She frowned and stared over Tammy's shoulder for a long moment. "Hmm. If he's moving, how can he start a new …" The rest of her mumbled words were drowned out by an announcement over the speaker.

Tammy's heart fell to her shoes. Michael Clark was married and moving away. Blood rushed to her cheeks. Then what had he been doing flirting with her last night when she knocked him down in the parking lot? He didn't have any more integrity than Ted. Her dream of getting to know him shattered in one fell swoop. "All right. Thank you, ma'am." She turned and walked out of the office. She couldn't bear to talk to Charlotte now.

*****

Tammy walked into the downtown bistro, glancing at the

blackboard with the daily offerings. Hmm. Caesar salad sounded good.

Joella sat at booth close to the window. At least she might be interested in some banquet tickets, the only bright spot of the noon hour.

Not only was Tammy saddened about learning Michael was married and moving away, Joella would probably talk about God the entire lunch. She waved at her sister and sat down in the booth across the table from her.

A wide grin appeared on Joella's face. "How are things at the hospital?"

Tammy attempted to dispel her dismal mood and pasted a smile on her face. "Very well. In fact, our department's going to be recognized by the El Camino Hospital Auxiliary Society at the annual banquet."

"That's impressive. You deserve it."

So far no religious talk. "Yeah. The head of the organization is the daughter of one of my patients who's now deceased. She was so impressed with the care her father received at the end of his life, a large percentage of the profits this year will go to geriatrics."

"That's a blessing."

Not a blessing, but the result of hard work on Tammy's part as well as the geriatrics staff. "I've got tickets if you'd like to purchase them."

Joella's face brightened. "I'll talk to JD, but I'm sure we will."

The waiter arrived at their table. "Yes, ladies. What can I get you?"

Tammy flipped open the long list of food choices then shut it again. "I'll have a Caesar and water with lemon."

"Make that two." Joella pushed the two menus to the edge of the table.

He smiled and scribbled on a pad of paper.

Tammy retrieved the napkin from the place setting and set it in her lap. "So, what have you been doing?"

"Keeping up with Baby Jacob is a fulltime job. Babies require a lot of energy, but I do manage to squeeze in some quiet time."

"So the little tyke occupies most of your day? How is my nephew?"

"Healthy, thanks to the Lord. God has truly blessed us with

our child."

Though religion meant so much to Joella, Tammy still couldn't embrace her sister's beliefs. There were too many questions that she hadn't reconciled. Why would a loving God send people to hell? Why did He allow suffering in the world? "You and JD are well-informed parents. That's the important thing."

"Thanks, but we praise God for a healthy baby who was born at term."

"I'm sure parents with children in the NICU would agree. Like the Reyes baby, many infants don't have the opportunity to grow in utero for the normal forty weeks."

Joella nodded and took a sip of water. "So have you met any cute guys lately?"

Tammy rolled her eyes. Undoubtedly her sister thought Tammy should be married and having a bunch of kids. "Not really. I'm concentrating on my career right now."

Resisting the urge to twiddle her thumbs, she fidgeted in her chair as Joella chatted on, describing how God worked in her life. But that was better than continuing the conversation about potential men in her life.

When the waiter set their salads, drinks, and two checks on the table, Joella bowed her head and said a blessing out loud.

After they'd lunched for fifteen minutes, Tammy finished her salad and checked her watch. "Sorry, Sis, but I've got to get back to work." She picked up her bill and rose.

Joella grabbed it from her hand. "This is on me."

"You don't have to but thanks. I appreciate it." Tammy blew a kiss and headed toward the door. Though Joella didn't quite come out and say Tammy should go to church again like she had when she was a child, her conversation about the Lord felt uncomfortable. She might as well have told Tammy she thought she was a heathen and needed to do something about it.

Tammy stepped into her Ford, started the ignition, and maneuvered toward the hospital along the city street, crowded with the lunch people returning to work. She drummed four fingers on the dashboard then flipped on the radio.

"For God so loved the world He gave His one and only Son." The familiar scripture she'd heard as a child. "Salvation is available through Jesus Christ our Lord."

She pressed her lips in a straight line and punched the button to change stations. She'd heard enough religious talk for one day. Why was it Christianity seemed to be the only topic of conversation for some people?

Chapter Five

Michael stood from the table and clapped Dad's shoulder. "Those steaks were grilled to perfection. Thanks, O master chef."

"I'm glad you could get off early this afternoon. Mom wanted me to cook out while we had plenty of daylight. She's planning on taking the boys to a movie later on this evening."

His sister, Alexus, pushed back her chair, gathered a few plates, and turned to their father. "I'm so glad you and Mom can be around my little guys before they get too old. The way kids grow these days, Jeremy and Toots will probably be in college before we can turn around."

Michael picked up a platter of leftover steak. "How in the world did your youngest son get a name like Toots?"

"You don't want to know." Alexus laughed. "Let's just say he had a digestion issue for a while."

Dad chuckled. "Well, it's such a pleasure to have my three kids all together under one roof again. And my rambunctious grandsons. I just wish your husband could've made the trip, Alexus."

"Oh, John can't get away from his architectural firm right now."

Still sitting at the table, Jeremy looked at his mother. "Mom, can we go play with the puzzles Grandma bought us."

"Yes you may, boys. But put your plates in the sink first."

"Yea." Each boy grabbed his plate and glass and headed toward the kitchen.

Mom rose from the table, picking up the empty bowl that held the salad.

"You go relax and play with the boys. I'll enlist my brothers to get the kitchen clean. Won't take but a minute," Alexus said.

"Count me out." Darnell headed toward the hall entryway. "I've got to get back to the office."

"I'm not an expert on cleaning up, but I'm willing to learn." Michael turned toward the kitchen and set the platter on the counter.

Alexus followed and opened the dishwasher. She called to Dad who'd trailed behind them. "You go on with Mom. Michael and I will get this." She glanced at him. "I've wanted to chat with you anyway."

"I won't argue with that," Mom said. She and Dad headed toward the living room behind their grandchildren.

As kids, Alexus had always looked after Michael when Mom was busy. Since she was ten years older, he'd thought of her as a second Mom. "I'd like to talk to you, too, about a project I'm working on." He returned to the dining room and cleared a few more serving dishes then walked back into the kitchen.

"Okay, but first things first. Are you dating anyone I need to know about?"

"Women. Life isn't all about romance, you know." Michael laughed. "No one right now." A vision of Tammy waltzed into his head. "There is a nurse…" No, he wasn't dating her. He'd only talked to her a couple of times. And she'd knocked him to the ground in the middle of a rainstorm. The corners of his mouth lifted.

"A nurse?"

"No, I don't know why I said that. To tell you the truth, I'm too involved in plans to build a children's hospital. One where premature babies can get top quality care with specialty equipment and services—a level IV NICU with the most acute care."

Alexus stopped rinsing dishes and gaped at him. "Michael, that's marvelous. I'm so proud of you."

What a different reaction from Darnell's. Alexus believed in him. The same way he hoped a wife would someday. By the time they finished stacking all the dishes in the dishwasher and wiped down the sink and counters, Michael had outlined the entire project for his sister.

She grasped his hand. "If there's anything, anything I can do, please let me know. In the meantime, the boys and I are coming over to your townhouse to spruce things up—like adding a woman's touch to your pad."

"You don't have to—"

"Shh. Don't tell, but you're my favorite brother. There will be no objections. In fact, we'll go right now so we can give Mom and the kids plenty of time to get to the theater." She cupped her hand around the side of her mouth. "Boys, come in here and give Grandma Clark a break for a couple of hours."

*****

Tammy checked the clock on the wall at the nurses' desk. Time for her to head home. She said good-bye to the night nurse and took the elevator to the employees' parking lot. After revving up her ten-year-old Ford Taurus, she pulled out into downtown traffic.

Stopping by Mildred's was next on her agenda. At the stop light, she reached for the button on the radio and pushed it off again. She didn't want to risk hearing any more of those religious programs that seemed to pervade the airwaves these days.

When the light turned green, she turned onto Pine. The street led north out of the city center and to the address Mildred gave her—an upscale neighborhood about five miles from Tammy's apartment.

After a few more blocks, she turned into the fashionable neighborhood. Driving along, she slowed as she glanced at the house numbers for the expensive townhouses. Two more doors down was Mildred's. After pulling into the driveway, she cut the engine and got out of the car.

Mildred waved from the window and in only seconds opened the front door. Strands of hair falling from her ponytail into her face, she blew a curl from her cheek and wiped her hands on old exercise pants. "I can't thank you enough." She handed over a manila folder."

"I'm happy to."

"You might know. The day before my vacation started I had

more than one incident I needed to write up. First I was helping a post-op patient walk from his bed to the bathroom, and he stubbed the big toe of his right foot on the IV pole. Then I found another patient trying to get on the elevator. She said she was looking for her dog." Mildred threw her hands up in an I-give-up gesture. "That's just for starters."

"I'll be happy to turn these in for you." Tammy chuckled and glanced around at the costly homes lining the street. "You certainly have a gorgeous house."

Mildred beamed. "We're blessed to live here." She pointed across the street. "One of the doctors from the NIC unit has a house over there. Michael Clark. In the spring, he spends time working in the yard. Though he's one of the finest doctors at El Camino General, he also has the best groomed lawn and flower beds in the neighborhood."

Tammy tensed. "Hmm. That's interesting." How ironic was that? Michael lived nearby, but seeing where he shared a home with a wife and kids sent a stab of pain to her chest. She glued her eyes on Mildred trying to avoid looking at his house. "Well, I hope you and your family have a great time."

"Thanks so much." Mildred gave Tammy a hug. "I'll return the favor soon." Walking back toward the house, she waved and then closed the door.

Tammy returned to her car but movement across the street caught her eye. Two little boys with curly hair who looked something like Michael ran around in the front yard of his light tan two-story townhouse. Then a well-dressed, stunningly beautiful woman opened the front door and called. "Boys, time to come inside now."

As if a boxer had fisted her in the region of her abdomen, she sucked in a breath. Michael's adorable children followed his wife inside.

An unbidden pang of regret hit her. Wasn't that her luck? Falling for an incredible guy who was already married?

When Tammy dismissed Ted from her life, she hadn't thought another thing about it. She was glad to get rid of him. But Michael? A guy who'd attracted her from the first day she'd met him in the doctor's lounge was married. Seeing his family only reinforced the fact.

As she drove home, the incident made her determined more than ever to pursue her advanced degree. She pulled into her apartment complex's parking lot and headed upstairs. She'd find plenty of information about a NP degree after a Google search.

Chapter Six

Tammy left her patient's room and sauntered down the hall to the nurses' station. After discovering Michael was married, the disappointment still hung on. No matter what she did, images of him and his family popped into her head. Even last night, she'd tried to distract herself by exploring options for enrolling in a nurse practitioner program, but that didn't help much.

Though her stomach growled, and it was time for her lunch break, she couldn't bring herself to eat now. She patted her pocket where the charity banquet tickets rested.

Instead of going to the cafeteria to get a bite to eat, Tammy took the elevator to the seventh floor and turned toward the nurses' station. Since she didn't stop to speak to Charlotte yesterday, she'd check with her now.

Charlotte sat at the desk peering at her computer screen. Her cheery friend with a head full of blonde curls looked up and smiled. "Hey, Tammy."

"Hi, Charlotte. Have you heard about the charity banquet? The hospital auxiliary is raising funds, which will benefit every department." She held out a packet of tickets. "Would you mind checking to see if anyone on your floor would like to participate?"

Charlotte pushed her glasses up on her nose and reached for the tickets. "Sure. Be happy to. Maybe we could go together. I've missed hanging out with you the way we used to in school."

Of course attending the event with Dr. Clark was out of the question, especially if he was married. "Sounds good. Let's do it.

Something else I wanted to ask you. Have you ever considered a nurse practitioner program?"

"I've thought about taking classes again, but honestly Tammy, I'm kind of burned out on school right now. Maybe someday. But I hear the onsite clinical practicum opportunity here at El Camino General is excellent. Are you considering it?"

"Yes, I applied at several schools that offer online classes and financial help."

"I admire your drive and determination." She giggled. "But right now I'm hoping to find a guy and settle down. We'll see."

"I was wondering. When you sell tickets to the doctors, could you encourage them to bring their wives? Like Dr. Clark." Before Tammy could call the words back, she'd opened her mouth, lowering her voice to barely a whisper.

A furrow creased Charlotte's brow. "Dr. Clark? He's not married."

Tammy froze. "Are you sure?"

Charlotte tilted her head to one side. "Yeah, why do you ask?"

She didn't have time to go into the whole story. "I heard he was. Are you positive?"

"Yes." Charlotte stuck a pencil behind her ear. "He's not even dating. I walked into the doctors' lounge the other day when he was talking about a project he's got going. After the nurse practitioner on duty, Jerry Taylor, jokingly asked him about his latest girlfriend, he said he didn't have time for dating or marriage." Charlotte put a finger to her mouth. "Shh. Here he comes now."

Tammy's heart pounded as she glanced up.

The handsome doctor approached at a brisk pace, looking as if intent on accomplishing a mission. When he arrived at the nurses' station, he smiled at Charlotte. "Do you have those files finished for me?"

"Sure do." Charlotte reached toward her inbox and handed him a couple of manila folders.

"Thanks." He turned to Tammy. "How's everything? Not stabbing guys in the chest with umbrellas these days, I hope."

Charlotte's eyes widened as she stared at them.

"No. I retired the treacherous weapon." Tammy tried not to stutter but couldn't disguise her wide smile.

Charlotte chuckled aloud.

"That's a relief." Michael's smile melted Tammy like warm wax.

"How's the Reyes baby?" Only thing she could think to say.

"I wish all my babies did as well. She'll probably be going home in another couple of days." He scratched his head. "Do you know the family?"

"Oh, in a roundabout way. My sister's husband is Dave Reyes' best friend. Really Joella and JD are closer to Betty Ann and Dave than I am."

"I understand Dave is a pastor." He switched the folders from one hand to the other.

"Yes, my sister goes to his church. She's active in the stay-at-home-mother's group." She wanted to ask him if he attended the church as well. Hard to tell if he was the type. "Do you—"

He glanced over her shoulder and checked his watch. "Excuse me, Tammy. The parents of one of my patients are here for their appointment." His lips parted as he held her gaze for a moment then walked in their direction. Greeting the couple, he shook hands with both then the young mother and father followed him down the hall.

Charlotte folded her arms over her chest and sported a knowing grin. "Care to tell me what that was about?"

Warmth crept up Tammy's cheeks. "Well, you see, there was a little accident in the parking lot the last time it rained. I speared him with my umbrella and knocked him down."

"Oh, wow." Charlotte raised an eyebrow. "Now I see why you were asking if he was married. Tammy Crawford, you should've seen your eyes when he came up. I think you've got a crush on him."

Tammy hiked her hands on her waist and smiled. "Nurse Sperry, you're crazy." She peered at Charlotte a moment. "Okay, maybe I do, but don't spread it around."

Again Charlotte place a finger over her lips. "Your secret is safe with me." She turned back to her computer screen then looked up. "Seriously, Tammy, I make it a practice not to repeat gossip. But if I might say, I think you've got good taste in men."

Turning toward the elevators, Tammy waved. Then she stopped in her tracks. If Michael Clark wasn't married, then who were those people she saw at his townhouse, and what did Iris mean when she said he was moving his family away?

*****

Michael walked into the seventh-floor doctors' lounge and poured a cup of coffee then carried it to his office. The hot java warmed his insides on the cold but sunny November morning. He hoped he'd run into the perky young nurse with the freckles across her nose once again.

"Well, good morning, Dr. Clark." His secretary's bright smile brought another ray of sunshine to the chilly day.

"Good morning, Iris. How's my favorite secretary today?" Though bouts of forgetfulness characterized her work more frequently, no great damage had occurred so far. Once she'd forgotten to write into the schedule an appointment she'd made for a patient's parents. Luckily he was in his office when they showed up. Then she'd allowed her inbox to overflow but stayed late to organize it. How could he criticize her? She'd become more like a grandmother to him than a secretary, and he didn't want to hurt her.

"I told my grandson about your project and your resolve to see it through. I think it helped to motivate him to study harder." She lifted a brow. "Just one question. Did you tell me you're moving your family away from El Camino? I think I get a little confused ever so often."

He laughed at the quizzical look on her face. "No. I'm not moving, and I'm certainly not married. I told you I would sell my townhouse if I had to and move in with my family. I meant my mother and father."

"Oh, I guess I told that young nurse—" The phone rang, and Iris reached to answer it. "Yes, Dr. Clark's office." She smiled. "Yes, Mr. Reynolds, we'll be happy to participate."

Michael headed toward his office and closed the door. Iris had to be nearing eighty. She'd probably been at the hospital since the day it opened. He only hoped he'd function as well when he reached that age. He edged down at his desk and opened his file with the hospital plans. "Hmm. Mr. Jamison. I wonder why he hasn't called back." Michael dialed his number.

"Jamison Investments. Mr. Jamison's office."

"Yes, this is Dr. Michael Clark. May I speak to Mr. Jamison.

It's in connection with an investment he and I had discussed."

"Yes, Dr. Clark." He heard the shuffling of papers. "He's out of the country and won't be returning for several weeks." A woman's voice relayed the message. "Let's see. There's a memo on your file. He says because you didn't return his call and confirm the meeting, he couldn't wait any longer. He'll be pursuing another investment overseas."

"Didn't return his call?" His mouth fell open. "When did he contact me?"

"Hmm. Four days ago. He left the message with your secretary. I'm sorry, sir."

"I was never notified. I'm surprised he didn't call my private cell number. Perhaps I neglected to give it to him." Moisture formed on his brow.

"I apologize for the confusion, sir."

"Thank you. Is there any way I can get in contact with him?"

"I'm afraid not. He doesn't publicize his personal cell number. Perhaps contact him again when he returns. I'd suggest sometime next month.

"Yes, I'll do that." With no other reason to continue the conversation, Michael hung up the office phone and walked back into the main office. He needed to clear up this situation. "Iris, did I get a message from a Mr. Jamison?"

"I don't think so." She cleared her gravelly voice. "Let me check through my inbox." Iris pulled papers out and scattered them around on her desk in a jumbled pile. Then her face reddened. "Oh, dear." She picked up a small scrap of paper. "I think this is it." She looked up at him, a frown knitting her brow. "I'm very sorry. It must've gotten buried in the desktop organizer."

Humph. She didn't keep her desktop organizer very organized. Heat filled Michael's neck, and he restrained the urge to say an unkind word to her. But anyone could make a mistake at any age, and Iris was too dear to him to hurt her feelings.

She spoke in a squeak. "I hope it wasn't too important."

"It was, Iris. Please be more careful next time." Surely, he'd find other investors. Michael went back in his office and slumped at his desk. He'd have to begin the funding process all over again.

Chapter Seven

Tammy peered out her apartment window. The last few leaves flew off the trees with the swirling wind. Hard to believe Thanksgiving had come and gone, and she still hadn't found the chance to get to know Michael better. Maybe she needed to forget about him. But the image of his deep brown eyes and lazy smile had accompanied her to sleep almost every night for weeks. She'd never been this fascinated with a guy before.

Only one bright spot remained—Charlotte swore Michael didn't have a wife. Tammy wouldn't be one hundred percent sure, though, until she heard it from his mouth, and what were the chances of that? She couldn't come right out and say, "Oh, by the way, are you married? Who were the woman and two kids I saw at your townhouse?"

She sighed and plopped down on the couch, picking up the pile of brochures on the coffee table. She thumbed through them one by one. Each provided information on the various programs available for nurse practitioner programs online. Losing concentration, she tossed them back. Maybe if she visited the doctors' lounge again on her break, she'd run into Michael.

Her ringing cell brought a needed diversion from her thoughts. "Hello."

"Hey, Tammy. This is Betty Ann Reyes. It was great seeing you a few weeks ago in the NIC unit."

"Hi, Betty Ann. How's Abby? Are you, Dave, and Alice adjusting to the new little person in your home?" Tammy wasn't sure if she could handle caring for a crying baby.

"I wouldn't be telling you the truth if I didn't say it's pretty tough around 3:00 a.m. Since I'm nursing, Dave can't help out with the feedings. But he's great with changing diapers. Alice is begging us to let her give it a try."

For one small moment, Tammy's previous thoughts about little ones seemed to fade as memories of Dave's little girl, Alice, invaded her mind. How she ran to Baby Abby's crib in the NICU once and sang to her.

A husband and children—someone to love who loved you. She gave her head a little tap. What was she thinking? She had a career. "Sounds like quite an adventure, Betty Ann."

"No doubt. Well, let me tell you why I'm calling. Next Sunday, we're having Abby's baby dedication at church then a buffet dinner afterwards at our house. I'd love for you to come. Joella and JD will be there."

Tammy liked the Reyes family and wanted to support them. She'd even endure a church service to spend time with them. "Sure, Betty Ann. I'd love to."

"Oh, and Abby's doctor will be coming as well. Dr. Clark."

As if she hadn't heard correctly, Tammy snatched the cell phone in front of her face and stared, then stuck it to her ear again. "Dr. Clark? That's cool. He takes a personal interest in his patients." Yeah, she'd heard correctly. She restrained the words *all right* that almost emerged from her mouth. "He's an excellent doctor. I've seen him at work a couple of times in the NICU."

"I have to agree. He saved our little Abby's life. Anyway, I hope you can come. The church service starts at eleven and the dedication will be at the end. You know where New Life is?"

"Yeah, I attended there once with Joella." She'd do it for Betty Ann and Dave. And best of all, she'd get to see the good-looking doctor.

Another consideration—she could find out if he did plan to leave the area. Long distance relationships hardly ever worked out, so if he intended to move, she'd be able to forget the notion of dating him. "See you soon, Betty Ann. I hope you get some sleep."

Betty Ann chuckled. "Thanks."

Tammy hung up the phone and strolled into her bedroom to her closet. Now what should she wear?

*****

Michael straightened his tie in the mirror of the men's room at New Life Fellowship. Though he appreciated an invitation from the Reyes couple for the baby dedication, he wondered if this church would be like Mom and Dad's new mixed congregation. As an adult, he always seemed to seek out an all-black church since he'd grown up in one.

The door squeaked and someone entered. He glanced behind him. Dave Reyes.

Dave slapped him on the back. "Hey, Dr. Clark. Thanks so much for coming today."

"Hi Dave. I'm Michael to you. Thanks for asking me. I enjoy getting more involved in the families' lives of the patients I treat. It's rewarding to see those premature babies catch up with their peers as they grow and develop."

Dave washed his hands in the sink and combed his hair. "We're honored you're here. I'd like for you to sit up at the front with our family and friends who've come for the dedication. And of course the buffet dinner at our house afterwards."

Feeling connected to this group of Christians energized Michael. He turned and followed Dave from the men's room through the foyer to the sanctuary. At the end of the aisle before the front of the church, the first several rows were filled with people. The aisle seat to the left sat empty, next to the red headed nurse with the freckles over her nose. His pulse's rapid beats surprised him. Not his usual reaction to women he worked with, but then Tammy Crawford had intrigued him since the first time he met her in the doctors' lounge. He slipped into the seat next to her.

She turned toward him with a smile and back to the worship team at the front of the church who had just begun to sing. When the pastor began the dedication, Michael realized he'd missed most of the church service. Awareness of the gorgeous, slender woman beside him, the scent of some kind of flowers swirling around his nose, had captured his attention for almost forty-five minutes.

Determined to pay attention to the baby dedication ceremony, he glued his eyes on the Reyes couple. They faced a man introduced as Pastor McNeely.

Dave clutched the hand of a child about seven or eight as Betty Ann cradled the baby in her arms.

For ten minutes, the pastor read from the Bible scripture that admonished the parents to raise their child with Christian principles. Then he cast his gaze on the couple standing in front of him. "Do you promise to provide for Abby's physical, emotional, intellectual, and spiritual needs?"

"We do." Dave and Betty Ann's voices blended as one.

What would it be like to have a close relationship with another person like Dave and Betty Ann had? A wife who cherished him and whom he loved as well?

Pastor McNeely lifted his face toward the audience. "Will the congregation please stand?"

Michael rose from his seat as Tammy and the rest of the family and friends stood. Her side brushed up against him when she rose, alerting his senses to her perfume once again.

"Do you, people of New Life Fellowship, recognize this child as a gift of God, and will you do your part in supporting these parents in raising little Abby in the admonition of the Lord?"

Michael opened his mouth to say *we do* with the rest of the people but shut it again. He wasn't a member of this congregation, but more than that, the realization came to him. He could care for a baby's body, but the thought of spiritually guiding a child baffled him.

*****

Michael followed the crowd down the aisle and into the foyer. He couldn't help but notice the way Tammy's silky Kelly-green dress clung to her feminine curves as she floated along in front of him. Auburn red hair fell around her shoulders, and four-inch heels added to her five-six frame, lengthening her shapely legs.

Joella met up with them in the foyer. "Dr. Clark, do you know the way to the Reyes home?"

He smiled down at the two sisters, both so different in appearance and in manner. Joella—dark haired and taller than Tammy. Tammy, a busy career nurse and Joella, a mom who didn't work outside the home. "How about you ride with me over there?" he asked Tammy. "That way I'll be assured not to get lost. I can drop you back at the church afterward."

"Sure." Tammy blinked green eyes that matched the color of her dress. "Since I rode with Joella and JD, I would just need a ride home."

Even better. "Consider it done."

"Great." Joella waved at them and turned toward a man approaching from a hallway leading into the foyer. He balanced a dark-haired toddler in his arms. "I'll see you both at the Reyes home."

Michael held the foyer door for Tammy as she drifted out in front of him. "My car's the blue Mercedes on the last row. Thanks for being my navigator."

Tammy's slow grin sent his pulse jumping again.

At the car, Michael held the door for Tammy as she slid long legs into the front seat. When he got in and started the motor, she turned to him.

"I don't mean to sound nosy, but I was wondering when you plan to move."

Michael pulled out of the parking lot, curious why she asked the question. "I'm not moving. What made you think I was?"

Her eyes widened as she laughed. "Oh, I suppose I heard it somewhere at the hospital."

"Never had the notion to move. I'm happy practicing medicine here at El Camino General."

"I understand. I believe I can achieve my goals here as well."

Goals that came first in her life? Did she think he put medicine above his relationship with the Lord? He didn't intend to give that impression. And what about Tammy? Where did God fit into her life?

Tammy crossed one shapely leg over the other. "Now that I've got the chance, I'd like to ask you a question."

Curiosity snagged him. "Shoot."

"What do you think of the nurse practitioner clinical program at the hospital? I'm seriously considering an advanced degree."

Michael gazed at the attractive woman sitting in the front seat of his car next to him. Besides beauty, she was smart and wanted to move forward in the field of medicine, his passion. "You might consider visiting the administrator's office. I've spoken with the person in charge several times. We've had NP candidates train in the hospital in a variety of clinics. The students are closely supervised, and the small student to faculty ratio is advantageous. The candidate has direct contact with the expert staff member in the appropriate field of advanced practice." He took a breath. "All that to say, we have an excellent program here in El Camino. I'd encourage you to enroll."

"You've confirmed my thinking." She pointed to the left. "Turn at the light. It's a straight shot from here."

After the turn, Michael said, "What field do you plan to pursue—geriatrics?"

"Yes. I've always felt a leaning toward that branch of medicine."

An established neighborhood he'd visited a couple of times came into view.

"It's the house on the next corner," Tammy said.

The closest spot to the Reyes's ranch-style home was several doors down. After grabbing the box wrapped in pink paper that contained the gift card, Michael strolled around to open the door for Tammy.

Her shorter skirt length revealed a portion of her slender thighs. He drew in a breath. What was wrong with him? He'd seen other women's legs before.

The feel of her smaller fingers against his skin captured his attention as Tammy grasped his offered hand when she stepped out the car. He couldn't remember when a woman enticed him more.

When they were greeted by Dave at the front door, Michael set the gift on a table in the entry way with other presents wrapped in various shades of color—yellow, pink, green. A baby car seat, a stroller, and a diaper bag with pink balloons attached rested on the floor near the table.

After chatting for about twenty minutes, hunger pangs attacked Michael, and he was grateful for Betty Ann's announcement that everyone should line up for the buffet dinner.

For desert, a warm brownie topped with caramel sauce and coffee ice cream completed the feast. When the guests began to depart, he approached Tammy in the living room while she chatted with a young lady JD had introduced as Glorilyn, his sister. "I see about half the crowd has left. Are you ready to go?"

"Yes, I think it's about time." She hugged Glorilyn. "See you soon." Tammy retrieved her purse from a side table and stopped next to him.

Glorilyn looked from Tammy to Michael, probably wondering if they were an item. Was that wishful thinking on his part?

Together they said their good-byes and ambled back to his car. On the way to take Tammy home, he mentally rehearsed what he'd say when they arrived. Pulling up in front of her apartment, he turned in the seat, facing her.

She seemed to study his face a moment then turned to open the passenger door. "Thanks for the ride home."

"One moment, Miss Crawford." He rushed around and held the door as she stepped from the car. "I'm not letting you go in before asking you. Would you do me the honor of having dinner with me tomorrow night?"

Emerald green eyes flashed as moist lips lifted in a smile. "I'd love to."

"Perfect. Give me your number, and I'll call you tomorrow about the time."

After Tammy told him her cell number, she studied his face. "Aren't you going to write it down?"

"Are you kidding? It's engraved on my brain now."

Chapter Eight

Tammy flipped through every item of clothing in her closet, scooting each hanger to the right a few inches so she could examine the next outfit. Tonight she wanted to wear the dressiest garment she owned. After all, Michael said they were going to Giorgio's downtown, the best Italian Restaurant in El Camino.

Her little black dress hung on the end. Okay, that would do. Black lace covered the nylon lining. The knee-length skirt clung to her hips, but the feature she loved the best was the revealing dip of the fabric on the back of the dress. Four-inch black leather heels and the diamond pendant Mom had given her before she died would highlight her look.

The fragrance of jasmine and sandalwood filled her senses as she showered with her favorite body wash. When Michael asked her to dinner last night, she couldn't believe she'd finally get to spend some time with him.

Yesterday at the baby dedication, awareness of Michael sitting next to her had stolen her thoughts. She'd been so distracted that if Dave had asked her what she thought of Pastor McNeely's message, she would've stuttered and mumbled some vague answer.

More than anything, learning that the attractive doctor wasn't married and didn't plan to move away excited her. Maybe the woman and children she saw at his townhouse were relatives. She'd try to find out tonight.

Tammy patted dry with the supersized, fluffy towel and misted herself with matching body spray, savoring the delightful aroma once again.

After slipping into house shoes, she shuffled to the bedroom. Last night as she'd drifted off to sleep, she'd pondered why she was so taken with Michael. At twenty-eight, she wouldn't be drawn in by a dazzling smile or deep brown eyes the color of rich earth. Then what was it about this man?

Michael's handsome face cavorted in her mind. He was a gentleman, and she respected him for his informative advice about the NP program, his playful manner after their collision in the parking lot, and his professionalism in treating a baby. His concern in attending to each case individually and his regard for colleagues showed.

The image of the infant in Dr. Clark's care the day she visited the NICU still captivated her. The doc held the helpless little life literally in his hands, using his training to improve the baby's start in the world.

She smoothed her dress on her hips and twirled around before the full-length mirror, approving of her appearance. While dating Ted, she mistakenly thought she wanted a guy she could manipulate. Now she realized things were different. She couldn't imagine trying to control the competent, skilled Dr. Clark—nor did she want to.

Her styled hair fell onto her shoulders in shiny auburn locks. The diamonds in Mom's necklace glistened in the bathroom lights as she attached the chain around her neck. Though she liked her reflection, would she make a good impression on Michael during their first date?

The short black leather jacket in the hall closet would work well. The doorbell rang as she slipped it on.

*****

During the drive to Giorgio's, Michael forced himself to pay attention to city traffic, but his gaze kept drifting to the gorgeous woman beside him. The subtle aroma of a flowery fragrance set his senses on fire. One look at Tammy's shape in the black lace dress which revealed slender legs elevated his pulse and kept it high.

He'd stewed over his own clothing, finally deciding on dressy jeans, a gray shirt and a blazer and tie, appropriate dress for

Giorgio's. He stole another look at Tammy and glanced back at the road. "Thanks for joining me tonight."

"I'm glad you invited me." She laughed. "I actually thought we wouldn't have this chance because I believed you were married."

"You said you heard the rumor at the hospital?"

"Oh, it was something your secretary said when I brought some tickets up to the Pediatrics floor."

Iris. No telling what kind of notion circulated in her head.

Tammy whispered. "I'm grateful you're not." The smooth tones of her luscious voice hinted of her likely attraction to him.

But did he really want a relationship right now? Especially, since he didn't know a lot about her.

In downtown El Camino, he turned onto Fifth which took them directly to Giorgio's. The restaurant had become one of his favorites after he met Darnell there once for lunch. "Giorgio's antipasto is excellent, and the lasagna's got an exquisite flavor—a touch of cinnamon with cheeses that blend to perfection."

Tammy chuckled. "You sound like a blurb out of a gourmet cooking magazine."

"I confess. I love Italian cuisine, the pastas, Italian salads and desserts—everything on the menu."

The trademark green awning with the brightly lit sign above announced that the restaurant was three more doors down. He stopped in front, passed his keys to the parking valet attendant in return for a ticket stub, then strolled around to open the door for Tammy. As many times as he'd been here, tonight felt like the first. Perhaps seeing it differently because of his lovely dinner partner.

The maître de greeted them. "Yes, sir."

"Clark. I made a reservation."

At the hostess station, the balding man in a dark suit scanned his computer screen. He looked up and smiled. "Yes, sir, a small table for two. Right this way."

Michael guided Tammy with a hand on her back as the host led them past the restaurant bar to an elegant dining room beyond. Like most fine dining establishments, the tables were covered with white tablecloths, and featured silver place settings and candle light. Classical music played in the background.

After the maître de seated Tammy and set leatherette-covered menus with the restaurant's name engraved in silver in front of them, Michael edged in across from her at the intimate table near the glass window.

She opened the book with the restaurant's offerings and scanned the pages. "So many choices, but I think I'll have an Italian salad."

With her wispy frame, he assumed Tammy wasn't a big eater. "At least let me tempt you with Italian rum cake or tiramisu later for dessert."

"Tiramisu sounds delicious." She sipped water from a long stemmed glass. "Rum cake. Hmm. I know the alcohol content is cooked away, but I'm not a fan of that flavor—or booze in general."

"I'm not a drinker at all. I've seen the damage it can cause in a person's life. To me, it's not worth the risk."

After they placed their order, which included a small antipasto as an appetizer, Michael handed the menu to the waiter and gazed at Tammy. Sparkles of light reflected from her eyes reminding him of leaves on newly budded trees in the spring. "Tell me more about your family. Do you have other siblings besides Joella?"

Long locks brushed her shoulders as she shook her head. "No, just the two of us. I've always wondered what it would be like to have a brother. How about you?"

"I'm the youngest in my family with two older siblings, my sister, Alexus, and my brother Darnell."

She lifted a brow and touched her cheek with one finger. "Do you have nieces or nephews?"

"Yeah, Alexus has two boys."

Glancing over his shoulder a moment, she grinned. "Does your sister live in El Camino?"

Why did Tammy seem so amused? "No, but she came for a visit before Thanksgiving. She assumed her sister mode and brought the boys over to my townhouse while she made it more livable. Gave it a woman's touch, she said. I suppose she thought my bachelor's pad needed help."

Tinkling of silverware and muted voices met Michael's ears as Tammy nodded with a grin, as if she understood Alexus's reason for sprucing up his townhouse. "Sounds like you've got a very caring big sister."

"She's the best." Michael rubbed the back of his neck. "Now, my brother is another consideration."

"What do you mean?"

"Oh, I suppose he's rather opinionated." He couldn't tell her the truth. Michael glanced up toward the entrance of the dining room. As if talking about Darnell had conjured him up, Michael's brother swaggered past the front of the room toward the restrooms. A lump formed in Michael's gut. Darnell's swaying gait indicated he'd been drinking heavily.

Michael scooted down farther in his seat, hoping Darnell wouldn't spot them. If he'd been drinking, he might not be good company. He turned back to Tammy. "So have you thought any more about your NP program?"

After the waiter delivered the appetizer, Tammy set her napkin in her lap. "Yes. I'm considering all my options. The first step will be to apply for financial help, but, hopefully getting a grant won't be a problem. My grades were good in nursing school."

"Impressive. You seem to be a goal-driven, hardworking career woman."

"Thanks. I have the same impression of you as a doctor." She lowered her lashes and raised them again. "I actually admired you from a distance when Joella and I visited Baby Abby in the NIC unit. Your caring approach toward your little patients is evident, Michael."

"My job is more important to me than I can say." Second only to God. He reached for her hand across the table, his gaze perusing Tammy's creamy white face.

"Well, brother. Who's your dinner companion? She must be a business acquaintance."

Michael released Tammy's hand and sat up straight. Just as he feared. Darnell had seen them. "Tammy, my brother, Darnell."

"Nice to meet you." Though she offered a pleasant smile, Darnell continued to scowl.

Darnell looked her over from head to toe. "I take it you must be a consultant assisting my brother with his hospital plans." The harsh tone grated on Michael as his brother swayed from one foot to the other.

Tammy squirmed in her chair. "No, I—"

"Tammy is a friend from the hospital and a nurse on the geriatrics floor." Michael cracked his knuckles. His brother's appearance at their table was as bad as the time in junior high when he tried to impress a girl with his ability to skateboard and fell on his face. He wanted to be anywhere except where she could see his clumsiness.

Darnell teetered a moment, his eyelids sagging. "Do you always take hospital employees out to dinner?"

"Look. We're merely having a quiet meal. I think you've been in the bar a bit too long." Michael stood. He couldn't allow his sibling to go back into the lounge now or to drive home. He turned to Tammy. "If you'll excuse me a moment, I'm going to call a cab."

Tammy nodded. "Sure."

After grasping Darnell's elbow, Michael steered his brother away from the table.

Darnell stopped, jerking free. "You need to watch the kind of company you keep. Especially white women."

No doubt Tammy heard that. Michael cringed. If he didn't get his brother out of the restaurant soon, he'd make an even bigger scene. He glanced at Tammy and mouthed the words. "I'm sorry."

After using his cell phone to call a cab, Michael gripped Darnell's arm until the yellow vehicle arrived at the curb. Stuffing him down into the backseat, he leaned closer. "Darnell, I know this probably isn't the time to remind you, but drinking is a costly and dangerous habit. I wish you'd stop." He slammed the door, anger welling inside. After he gave the driver Darnell's address, he walked back inside shaking his head.

When he arrived at the table, he edged into his chair. "I apologize for him. I'm afraid he drinks too much."

A furrow creased Tammy's brow as she gripped her hands together on the table. "Michael, is he upset because he saw you with a white woman?"

Chapter Nine

The wall calendar in Michael's office displayed the last month in the year. He shook his head with the incredulous thought. December had come and a new year would soon be upon him. He leaned back in his high-backed leather chair and rested his palms on his knees. Would the coming year bring the completion of a pediatrics specialty hospital to El Camino, and how would things with Tammy progress?

The spectacle Darnell made at Giorgio's made him flinch every time he thought about it. Tammy's question about his brother's behavior at seeing them together still preyed on his mind. Darnell hadn't only been drunk, he'd displayed his belligerence.

His sibling resented her because of the color of her skin, but Michael didn't want to tell Tammy. If he could pound some sense into his brother's thick skull, he would. So many times Mom had told them both that it's not the color of a person's skin but who they are inside. Hadn't Darnell gotten the message?

Of course, Mom's religious beliefs were the underlying source for her remarks, but Michael agreed with her. People didn't ask to be born with blue or black eyes, straight or curly hair, brown or white skin.

Mankind should cherish the person God made them to be. He formed each individual into a unique creature, loving them individually. Tammy couldn't be criticized for who she was any more than Darnell could be faulted for his ethnicity.

He folded his arms over his chest and leaned back farther in the chair. In reality, Darnell probably believed that, too. He merely didn't want Michael out with a woman of a different race. A race he felt continued to abuse and dominate other races to this day.

Michael straightened his back and leaned forward again. He didn't have time to worry about Darnell now, and who knew whether his brother would change his opinions? Michael needed to take advantage of his few free minutes. He picked up the folder on the side of his desk and flipped it open. After an Internet search for articles on the advantages and disadvantages of buying an existing building versus going the construction route, he copied off the most pertinent ones and filed them in the folder. Next he checked the availability of buildings currently for sale and made documents for his reference including a few promising local real estate offices.

Swiping a hand over his mouth didn't relieve much of the frustration when he thought about losing Mr. Jamison's potential investment. But Michael had to move forward. He'd have to search for other investors now. As soon as he set up his possible board of directors, they could help with that as well.

Before he'd thought it through, he pulled out his cell and called Tammy's number. The notion of seeing her again tonight made him feel alive.

"Hi, Michael."

"Tammy, do you have a second?"

"Yes. I haven't started rounds yet." She answered in a singsong voice. "Still working on paperwork at the nurses' station."

Sounded like Tammy was happy to hear from him. The sound of her voice gladdened his heart as well. "If you're free later on, do you want to go jogging in the park downtown? It's not too cold today, and besides we'll warm up when we get moving."

"Actually, that sounds like a great idea. I think I put on a few pounds at Giorgio's, though the tiramisu was worth it."

Michael couldn't stop smiling. "Was that the only thing about the evening that was worth the extra weight?"

"I can think of other things." She lowered her voice. "I loved having dinner with you."

Yes, but did she enjoy meeting his drunken brother and listening to his unkind remarks? "Great. Meet you at five-thirty on the south end of the park. We can access the walking trail from there."

She sighed. "I can't wait."

"Bye, Tammy," he whispered. Darnell would disapprove of him dating Tammy, but his mom wouldn't. Thankfully she was a fair person who embraced a Christian worldview and would support him. He still wasn't completely sure where Dad stood.

Darnell's unbending outlook grated on him. Michael frowned. Surely his brother wouldn't try to come between him and Tammy.

*****

Tammy parked next to the sign that said El Camino City Park. A few feet in front of her, the dirt-packed walking trail led around the entire area. She chuckled when she remembered the beautiful woman at Michael's townhouse, the mystery now solved. The children were his nephews and the lady his sister. She breathed out a sigh of relief.

Thoughts of Michael's sister morphed to his brother Darnell. The guy obviously objected to Michael having dinner with Tammy because of her race. Would Mr. and Mrs. Clark feel the same? And what would Joella and JD think about a relationship with Michael? Though she wanted to believe she didn't care what her sister or husband thought, she did.

She punched the button for the MP3 player, and sat back in the seat as Roberta Flack crooned "The First Time Ever I Saw Your Face." She melted as an image of Michael eased into her mind. The classic had been a favorite from the time she was a teenager. In high school she dreamed of who her special guy would be, and Ted had never been him. After college, though, she'd begun to think she didn't need him, whoever he was. Could she be changing her mind again? If she fell in love with Michael, how would that affect her career?

Michael drove up in his azure Mercedes and parked behind her. He slipped off sunglasses, opened the door, and smiled, even more attractive in casual clothes. The jacket of his jogging suit, the same color as his car, fit tightly over his muscular shoulders and arms. Without his white lab coat or a suit and tie, he seemed out of character—another side of Michael she'd enjoy getting to know.

She stepped out of the car and threw her purse into the trunk.

"Just because you're wearing those nice jogging clothes doesn't mean you're as fit as I am. I hope you can keep up."

Michael laughed. "You wish. Let's see if you're as tough as you think you are."

"Hey." She tapped his shoulder. "I take that as a challenge." Tammy set out on the trail.

"Wait. We've got to warm up first." Michael stepped over to the grassy area, now straw-brown.

"You're just delaying the inevitable."

The crook of his eyebrow over smoldering eyes set her nerves ablaze as his index finger wiggled a *come-here* gesture.

He didn't have to ask twice. "Okay, you're right." Tammy jogged over to him.

"See, I'm right about most everything." He tapped his chest with his fist.

Tammy smiled and followed him in a few leg stretches.

After five minutes, Michael looked toward the path. "You ready now?"

"Okay, let's go." Tammy took a deep breath.

"Stand next to me, and I'll count us off." He dug a straight line in the dirt path. "We'll go four times around."

"No problem." Tammy bent with palms on her knees. Michael couldn't be in better condition than she. She'd always prided herself in her athletic ability.

The hunky guy got into position next to her. "Get on your mark, get set." He cocked his head toward her and laughed.

"Okay, okay. I'm ready."

"Go." Michael called and started out in an easy jog.

The sweet smell of victory raced Tammy's spine when she passed Michael on the dirt path. She could beat this guy.

After three lengths around the large city block, Michael still remained a short distance behind her. As they headed into the fourth lap, Tammy started to huff and her side ached. If she didn't stop a moment and catch her breath, she'd fall over.

Michael whizzed past her and jogged backward, a smirk on his face. "Well, Miss Tammy, are you ready to admit defeat?"

Though she loved their teasing banter, she had to stop for a rest. "Yeah, but I'll be asking for a rematch after a few workouts at the hospital gym."

He jogged back toward her. "Just wondering if your red nose is as cold as mine." He placed the back of his hand on her nose and nodded. "Yep, it is."

Focusing on his face, she laughed. "Yours is red, too."

"Actually I'd say it's probably more like bright bronze."

She slipped her hand in his. "You're attractive no matter the color of your skin." The words slipped out of her mouth, but she didn't regret them.

As if trying to discover a hidden meaning behind what she said, he searched her face then his eyes dipped to her lips.

Michael's T-shirt expanding against his chest stole Tammy's breath—more than the vigorous run. He trailed a thumb down the line of her chin. "Your skin is beautiful, too, Tammy. Your whole face."

Not disguising the wide smile, Tammy strolled by Michael's side as they walked back to their cars. He'd asked her out. Now it was her turn. When she arrived at her Ford, she leaned against it and rollicked in the intensity of his gleaming dark eyes. "Do you like Mexican food? I was thinking about cooking up a fiesta next weekend."

A bright smile spread over his face. "I love tacos, enchiladas, chalupas. Count me in."

"Don't worry. I'm a pretty good cook." Tammy waved good-bye, fired up her ignition and pulled out onto the street beside the park. In her rearview mirror, she watched Michael slip on his sunglasses again and follow her for a couple of blocks.

When she put on her left blinker and turned, he smiled and waved as he continued down the street.

If she didn't want her heart taking the next leap, she'd better back off. But looking inside, she knew the truth. He captivated her.

*****

Still energized by his vigorous jog yesterday evening, Michael sank into his office chair. Tammy. He smiled when he thought of her determination and vigor to stay up with him. He'd tell her one of these days that he'd been a sprinter in college and even now ran whenever he had the chance, mostly on weekends.

Tammy's soft green eyes filtered into his memory. *Okay,*

Clark. You've got it bad. For a moment, he didn't want to believe the message in those words. His grandparents probably would've frowned on a dating relationship with her, though now Grandpa and Grandma Clark had passed away. He still wasn't completely sure what Mom and Dad would say, but he had the right to make his own decisions.

More important than anything—he needed to consider Tammy's connection with the Lord. How often had his mother spoken about the significance of marrying a Christian girl?

Michael booted up his computer and once again remembered Iris's grandmotherly smile she'd offered when he arrived at the office this morning. Today, she'd said she was praying for him and the building project. The assurance comforted him. Now at least three people were praying besides himself—Mom, Alexis, and Iris.

With several minutes left before time to make rounds, he'd take a look at the building project folder. He opened the top drawer where he kept it during the day. Though at night he usually stuck it in his briefcase and worked at home, he remembered, last night he'd forgotten it. Had he been distracted by his date with Tammy?

No folder. Since he'd added some documents yesterday and forgotten to put it in his briefcase, he probably left it on the desk or in the filing box last night before he went home. He scanned the top of the desk. The folder peeked out from under a medical book. He grasped the edge of the manila file and pulled it out, chiding himself for being careless.

He flipped it open and ran his hand across his hair. No papers. Nothing more than an empty wrapper. But where were the copies of his plans?

Maybe they'd fallen out in the drawer. He took everything out and went through each item. Nothing. He did the same with the second and third drawer. Then he investigated every inch of the top of the desk, the book cases, and the side desk. Nothing.

So far he'd identified several people who might be on a board of directors, explored the differences in building versus purchasing an existing building, and made a list of available structures. Of course he'd have to start back at point zero to find an investor. Was he supposed to again accumulate the information? His heart sank. Was he back to square one?

He opened the door to his secretary's adjoining office. "Iris."

He held up the empty folder. "Have you seen any papers on the building project that might've fallen out of here?"

Scrutinizing the item in his hand, she frowned. "No, no, Dr. Clark. I can't say I have."

Michael never felt helpless and out of control, but now the emotions threatened. "The file is here but the papers are missing."

"Oh, Doctor. I'm so sorry." Iris crept up from her desk. "Could they have found their way onto my desk?" She slowly investigated each desk drawer and stacking file then shook her head.

Another check on his desk produced nothing. He meandered back into the main office where Iris continued to look around.

He was almost running out of time to search. "You're sure you don't remember seeing them. My Internet work, list of board of directors, papers like that."

She paused and placed her finger on her temple. "No. I do remember the custodian asking me about some papers he found on the floor near your desk."

"The custodian?"

"He said he found wadded up papers on the floor and asked if he should dispose of them." She placed a crooked finger bent by arthritis to her temple. "Hmm. I think he said they were wadded up. Well, I figured you were writing another report for that medical journal you contribute to every month and needed to start over, crumpling up the discarded copies." She took a breath. "You know my grandson, the one who's in college. When he's working on an essay for his English class, he winds up with a pile of papers that reach to the top of the desk before he gets one he likes."

Michael's patience was quickly dissolving. As much as he loved her, he didn't have time to stand around and listen to stories about her grandson. "Look, Iris. I've got to get to rounds now. Will you please keep a watch out for them?"

She grinned. "Sure."

Michael started for the door leading down the hall to the UNIC. "Wait, Dr. Clark. I just remembered something else. Yesterday afternoon after you left, I went into your office to set some mail on your desk. I believe I saw the folder for your building project. As I reached toward your desk, the tremors got the best of me, and my hand shook. I knocked the folder on the floor."

"Iris. And you're just now remembering this?"

As if he'd struck her, a look of hurt appeared on her face. "I'm sorry. I picked up the folder but everything inside fell again. It pained me to bend over, but I gathered up all the documents." She placed a hand to her temple. "I think I did." She grimaced. "Oh, where's my memory these days?"

The picture became clear. The contents of Michael's folder had been swept away into the janitor's bin. He blew out a frustrating breath. Now he'd have to copy all the information from his computer again. He shook his head. His elderly secretary tested his composure. But did he have the heart to fire her given her financial situation?

WHAT GOD KNEW

Chapter Ten

Tammy checked her patient's vitals and finding them steady, marked the chart and stepped out of the hospital room. She exhaled the breath she'd been holding. The eighty-three-year-old woman's blood sugar had stabilized, and the doctor would probably send her home in a couple of days.

A growling stomach usually indicated hunger, but Tammy's appetite had disappeared. If she didn't each something, though, she couldn't keep up her strength.

She checked her watch. Almost time to meet Joella at the bistro again. Getting away from the hospital environment for a while energized her for the rest of the day, and she'd jumped at the chance when her sister called.

The assigned locker in the employees' room held her purse. She trekked down the hall to get her keys.

She and Joella were drawing closer as sisters, something Tammy welcomed. As children, they were never good friends. She'd always felt judged and unaccepted by Joella, but things had begun to change in the last several years. Joella had become more of a pal. If she'd only keep her religious opinions to herself, Tammy would be happy.

The quaint, downtown restaurant was only a few blocks from the hospital. She drove to the bistro, parked, and headed for the front door.

Outside tables were empty now but would be filled to the brim during the spring and summer. Through the picture window, she glimpsed Joella at a table toward the back and waved. Walking through the entrance, she made her way to the rear of the restaurant.

"Hey, girl." Joella smiled as Tammy took the seat across the table from her. "How's your day going?"

Jazzy music filtered through the room filled with other diners. "Good." Then she remembered the banquet. "Did you decide to go to the hospital auxiliary fund raiser?"

"Sure. I already told JD about it." Joella reached for her purse on the other chair. "It's a good cause. Give me four. I'll see if Betty Ann and Dave can get away."

"Thanks, Sis." She produced the tickets. "I promised to sell as many as I can. We're all excited on our floor. Geriatrics will receive special recognition."

"Cool." Joella passed Tammy cash then stuck the tickets in her purse. "Has a special someone asked you to the banquet?"

"No." Michael hadn't asked, but then she didn't say anything about it to him either. "Charlotte Sperry and I plan to attend together."

"I know you're a busy career woman, but I hope you'll find the love of your life one of these days. I know Ted wasn't him, but I hate to think of you all alone."

Tammy wasn't alone. She had a friendship with Michael. Maybe this was the time to tell Joella. She twisted her hands in her lap. Hopefully Joella would react differently than Darnell Clark. "I...er, it's interesting you should bring this up now. There's something I want to talk you about."

Joella narrowed her eyes. "You can share anything with me, Tammy. You know that."

The waiter set the drinks on the table and took their order for sandwiches. As if she'd already sipped a couple of swallows from the steaming chamomile tea, warmth filled her chest. "I've had a couple of dates with a guy lately. He's a doctor in the neonatal clinic." She giggled. "He's actually Abby Reyes' physician. You met him the day of the baby dedication."

"Hmm." Joella paused as if searching her memory. "Oh, yeah." She peered at Tammy. "I do remember ... "

"He's terribly handsome, smart, and single."

Again, Joella paused. "That guy has charisma and looks. And

a great career. But my only concern would be whether or not he follows Jesus as his Savior?"

Discussing Michael Clark with Joella might prove uncomfortable. Joella always had a way of bringing religion into everything. Her sister believed that unless Michael was a Christian, Tammy shouldn't consider him. But how could she screen her boyfriends by that criterion? She didn't believe in the faith herself.

*****

Tammy propped her feet on the coffee table and focused on her fuzzy pink house shoes then clicked on the TV. Lunch with Joella today had initiated a river of thoughts that hadn't stopped flowing. Before she'd met Michael, she'd never worried about a guy's religious affiliation. But for the first time, she'd found a man she could get serious about, and Joella said he needed to be a Christian. If he wasn't, would she and JD accept him—even if she didn't profess to be a believer?

Large crowds and sounds of people yelling drew her attention to the TV screen. The same event she'd seen earlier in the doctors' lounge before leaving the hospital was still the focus of several major news channels. Riots in a number of US cities had broken out, motivated by the shooting of a young black man who died in the back of a police vehicle after being apprehended.

This morning, news people reported that protestors demanded justice for the teenager. Yet not only did they express raw emotions, many had looted businesses, burned down a senior center, and shouted profanity against law officials. From the looks of it, they were still at it as police tried to control the crowds.

A man with brown skin standing next to another man, both neatly dressed in suits, caught Tammy's attention. She raised the volume on the TV.

The first man spoke. "I was once one of those angry young men. Though my mom did the best she could, I was raised in a one-parent home with two other brothers and didn't have a dime in my pocket. Back in the late sixties I looted, rioted, and protested. When someone knocked out the front display window of a shoe store, those new tennis shoes tempted me, and I grabbed a pair." He looked directly into the camera. "Then one day, God came into my life and changed me. Now I'm a pastor. My congregation built that senior center the rioters burned down. But that won't stop us from rebuilding. We did it once. We'll do it again."

Tammy bolted up and paced the floor. The man had obviously changed from an angry young boy to a mature man dedicated to helping people. He claimed God changed him. She flipped a piece of hair out of her eyes. Should she believe that or had the man merely come to his senses and matured?

She collapsed on the couch again. People didn't have the right to loot stores, but how would she have felt if her brother or boyfriend had died in a police wagon? So many questions and very few answers. She bit her lower lip then answered her ringing cell. "Hello."

"Is this the world's second fastest jogger?"

The sound of Michael's masculine voice on the other end of the line thrilled her. "So you're the first, I take it?" she laughed.

"Of course. And the first fastest wants to see the second. Can I pick you up for a cup of coffee?"

Before she spoke, she knew her answer. "I'd love to."

*****

In Starbucks, Michael gazed into Tammy's verdant green eyes and smoothed his hand over hers. He needed to face the facts. He was falling for her and fast. Still, he had no idea how she felt about him—or about God. He squeezed her hand and smiled. "There's something I want to talk about."

She seemed to search his face. "Sure. I hope everything's okay."

He sat back and took a sip of coffee, weighing the wisdom of asking her the question preying on his mind. Yet he needed to pull away before he'd completely lost his heart to her if she didn't want to spend any more time with him. "Tammy, let me get to the point. Does dating me, a man of another race, scare you?"

With folded fingers, she gazed at her lap, her mouth pressed into a straight line.

Michael's hopes fell to his shoes. He'd assumed that she might be falling in love with him, too. That a deeper relationship would be something she wanted. He shook his head. From what he'd observed, Tammy didn't seem like she'd allowed their different races to affect her feelings, but then maybe she didn't feel anything for him at all.

"Don't answer that." He downed the last of the coffee and stood. "Just pretend like I never asked."

She glanced up at him, a frown on her face, and she gasped. "No, Michael." She reached for his hand. "Please sit back down. It's nothing like you might be thinking. I've had a terrible teenage crush on you since the first day I met you in the doctors' lounge."

Now he felt like a stupid little kid. Michael slowly eased back in his seat. If he lost his confidence that quickly on the job, he'd be a failure as a doctor. He'd avoid that defensive attitude in the future. "Say that again?"

"I very much want to be with you, Michael. To see where this goes." She gripped his hand. "But what about your brother and the way he feels about me?"

Michael didn't live life to please his brother, especially when his views were bigoted. "I'm not worried what he thinks."

"Okay, but do you suppose he'd try to come between you and your family on the issue?"

"My mother especially understands where he's coming from and doesn't agree with him." He smoothed his hand over hers. "Tammy, it's something we can put out of our minds."

She gazed over his shoulder and back to him. "I trust your views, Michael, but have you seen the reports about the rioting? I hear the anger in those young voices when they protest or push themselves in front of the camera. Could Darnell be like them? Could he hate me because of the color of my skin?"

"Darnell is a successful man." Michael let out a long slow breath. "He runs a non-profit that helps the indigent with housing. He might be opinionated, and he has a big mouth, but he's not like those people in the street. I do have some distant cousins who were involved in the recent riots as gang members. Everyone has people in their families they're not proud of. I'm sure you have someone in your family who misses the mark, don't you?"

She stayed silent a moment then shook her head, a mischievous smile playing at the corner of her lips. "Nope, everyone in my family is perfect."

"Ha." He'd never get tired of her teasing or her little

mannerisms, like the way she played with the napkin in her lap. He traced the shape of her chin with his index finger. "My parents and my sister will adore you." Their gazes intertwined as his hand slipped up her arm.

"Michael, I...I would love to get to know you better."

He leaned across the table and kissed her cheek then allowed his lips to slowly travel to her mouth. Moments later, he sat back in his chair breathless. "Starbucks isn't the best place to kiss you." He laughed.

Chapter Eleven

Michael reached around Mom and Dad and held the heavy wooden door open then followed them inside the brick structure. Going to church with his parents was not something he ordinarily did. People in their congregation might worship in a different manner than the energetic bunch where he went, but did that matter? God was still God, and He never changed.

In reality, after his mom invited him to come to services and Sunday dinner, he hadn't thought much about it until today. His mind had been occupied with thoughts of the curvy nurse with the auburn hair and freckles over her nose.

A long center aisle divided wooden pews on either side of the sanctuary. At the front a lighted cross on the wall behind the pulpit drew his attention. Mom said they enjoyed the small church because everyone knew each other, unlike his larger one.

Dad led the way and stopped toward the middle. He scooted into a row on the left, Mom sitting by him and Michael near the aisle.

A choir filled the seats behind the pastor's pulpit as a song leader led the congregation in several tunes from the hymnal, plus a few Michael hadn't heard before. The traditional worship stood in contrast to the lively, spirited service where he attended.

Michael lifted his voice joining in with the rest. Though he'd anticipated feeling ill at ease, he relaxed when he witnessed the reverent expressions on peoples' faces, including those of his parents.

Then the music director shuffled through the hymnal. "Please turn to page three hundred twelve, 'Bless Be the Tie that Binds.' Concentrate on the words as you sing."

The swell of the organ's tones joined with jubilant, if off-key, worshipers. "Blest be the tie that binds, our hearts in Christian love, the fellowship of kindred minds is like to that above."

In his church, some people clapped loudly in time with the music, others shouted out praise to the Lord.

Today as his parishioners belted out the second verse, part of the words caught his attention. "Our fears, our hopes, our aims are one, our comforts, and our cares." That summed up the message of the hymn and addressed the few doubts he'd had about the service. Kindred minds in fellowship. These people sang of God, no different than the men and women who worshiped the Savior where he went to church.

After the choir took their seats, the preacher, dressed in a tailored black suit, rose from the first row and stood behind the pulpit. "Brothers and sisters in the Lord, I greet you in the name of the Lord Jesus Christ. Please open your Bibles …"

Michael grinned. He'd questioned the dissimilarities in his church and this one, but God resided here, too. He glanced at Mom. A pad and pen lay on her lap.

For twenty minutes, the pastor continued. "God loved mankind so much He sent His Son as a sacrifice for us. Not just for a certain group of people, but everyone. God cares about you, young or old, rich or poor, black or white, male or female. He's no respecter of persons."

It became plain. God cherished His people in all Christian denominations.

When the congregation rose and began gathering Bibles, Michael strolled out with his parents.

Arriving in the foyer, Mom patted his arm. "You're coming to lunch, right? We're having your favorite—roast, mashed potatoes, corn, and lemon meringue pie for dessert."

His stomach growled. His mother's cooking always won him over.

*****

Michael patted his full stomach and followed his parents into the comfortable living room.

Mom eased down next to him on the long, fabric-covered couch facing the fireplace, the cheery flames warming the room on the chilly day. "Honey, I'm so glad you had some spare moments to go to services with us." She patted his knee. "Spending time with you at home is a treat. Your Dad and I are very proud of how hard you've worked to become a doctor and pleased with your faith in God."

Dad stood in front of the blazing warmth rubbing his hands. Then he reclined in his easy chair across from the couch. "I suppose the army shaped much of my thinking, but Mom and I always raised you boys to understand the importance of personal integrity, and I can see that in your life."

He relished his parents' affirmation but couldn't take the credit. To be raised in a two-parent home where both mother and father were engaged in the childrearing process made a big difference. If he ever parented an offspring, he'd want that same structure. "Unfortunately, so many youth, no matter their race, didn't have the opportunities Darnell, Alexus and I had. Especially kids like those in the riots I've been following on TV. That could've been me if it hadn't been for you two."

Dad crossed an ankle over his knee. "A lot of those youth feel they've been singled out by police where their white counterparts are given a pass."

"I know that feeling." Michael blew out a frustrated breath. "A few years ago, I walked into an upscale department store looking for a couple of dress shirts. I found some designer ones and began thumbing through. I suppose I didn't look very professional in my T shirt and jeans. I happened to glance over my shoulder and a woman with a nametag including the store's logo stood behind me, her hands folded over her chest."

Mom gasped. "What happened then?"

"For a moment, I got mad. Then I asked her which ones she liked best. She looked horrified and pointed at one of them. I told her thanks and took it to the counter to pay for it. She watched me the entire time."

Dad raised his voice. "That would've angered me, too."

"But here's the funny part. The next week I stopped by after work to get a birthday gift for my colleague, Dr. Valentine. I walked up to the counter in men's colognes, and the same clerk worked behind the counter. I'd forgotten to take off my nametag that said Dr. Clark, neonatal specialist and was dressed in work attire. She glanced at the nametag and turned scarlet. She actually apologized for her actions before. What an amazing chance to witness to her. I explained that I could never take anything that wasn't mine because it would displease God. You should've seen her face then. Red as a ripe tomato."

Mom laughed. "God truly can work all things for good. Some people look at the color of a man's skin, but God sees our hearts." She stroked Michael's arm. "As I watched news coverage of the riots last night, a gentleman said it all. He spoke about his youth when he'd been one of those rioters, looting stores and filled with anger. Then he looked directly into the camera and said that God had made all the difference in his life. Now he's a pastor of a church that built the senior center looters had burned down. With a gleam in his eye, he promised that he and his parishioners would do it again."

Michael stared at his mother pondering her words. What could've changed the angry young man to a mature servant contributing in a positive way to his community? No doubt faith in God. "Your beliefs aren't about religion but reality, the difference God makes in a person's life."

Mom giggled. "Well, we haven't solved the world's problems today, but I pray our conversation has been meaningful to you."

He leaned toward his mother and kissed her cheek then looked toward Dad. "Thanks for dinner. I love you both. Dad, it was good to go to church with you today." His parents cared for him, but would that same acceptance extend to his choice of a mate if she was white?

Chapter Twelve

All the way to Tammy's, Michael's taste buds reminded him of the promised south-of-the border cuisine. He parked his Mercedes in front of her apartment building located in a neighborhood north of the hospital. The structure, an elegant four-story brown brick typical of the early nineteen hundreds, featured at least twenty units.

Engraved over the main entrance, letters spelled *Henrietta Building*. Choosing the stairs instead of the elevator, he juggled the poinsettia and the bag of chips and jar of salsa. The well-designed marble steps led to the second floor and Tammy's dwelling.

On her floor, six apartments wound around on either side of the hall. He strolled down the corridor, glancing to the right. Apartment 225. Pressing the antique brass doorbell, he waited. Like Tammy, her home spoke of her bold but fresh personality.

The woman who'd captured his thoughts for weeks opened the door, a smile on her lips.

Tight jeans hugged her hips, and an emerald blouse highlighted the green flecks in her eyes. "Hi, Michael."

Something about the way her lips moved as she said his name fascinated him. He held the poinsettia out to her. "Merry Christmas. Oh, and here's something to go with the meal."

Her eyes lit with pleasure as she grasped the flower and the plastic bag. "Thanks. Come on in."

The living area was small but tastefully decorated. A blue and white striped couch matched a white coffee table with a decorative arrangement of flowers. A tree with twinkling silvery lights stood in one corner. The soft sounds of seasonal tunes met his ears. He glanced at the painting on the wall. "I see you're a fan of contemporary art. That's a nice Kenneth Noland."

"I have to confess it's a print. I couldn't afford an original." She walked into the small kitchen visible from the living area and separated by a high counter with two bar stools. After opening the salsa, she poured it into a small glass bowl and smiled at him. "I didn't see you at the charity banquet last night. We had quite a turnout."

"I hated to miss it but one of my preemies showed signs of apnea and stopped breathing. I almost lost him, but he's going to make it."

"I'm so glad, Michael. You place your work above all else." She lowered her eyelashes. "I admire that in you."

"Thank you." If he were to guess by her tone of voice, her words weren't mere flattery but sincere. "So how did the banquet go?"

"I believe the auxiliary raised a healthy sum for the hospital."

"That's good to hear." Fund raising. Something he'd have to start thinking about as plans for the pediatric hospital fell into place.

She set the salsa and chips on the bar. "Dinner's ready. Hope you're hungry."

The aroma of chili powder, cilantro, and lime made his stomach growl. "I am. Looks like you don't need help with anything."

"Nope. Just sit down at the bar. I'm dishing up our plates now. Is iced tea okay?"

"Great." Michael relaxed into the high-backed, scooped chair and watched Tammy fill brightly colored ceramic plates with tamales, enchiladas, Mexican rice, and avocado salad. When she sat down beside him, he folded his hands. "Shall I say grace?" An automatic response before a meal.

Tammy gazed at him a moment then bowed her head. What was she thinking? Was praying before meals a custom in her life?

"Lord, please bless this food to our nourishment and the hands that prepared it." Lifting his head, he glanced at Tammy. Her eyes remained closed for a second longer then she directed her gaze to him, as if a question ran through her mind.

"Thanks." She picked up her fork.

After thirty minutes, Michael finished the heaping helpings Tammy had served, and she had managed to down about three quarters of her plate—the most he'd ever seen her eat.

"Would you like flan and coffee now or later?" She winked. "I have a feeling you'll say later if you're as full as I am."

"Definitely later." He piled his fork and knife on his plate. "Can I help with the dishes?"

She shook her head as she cleared their plates and put them in the sink. "I'm not going to worry about them now, just let them soak for a while. Let's sit in the living room and listen to holiday music." She punched a button on the CD player. "I never get tired of looking at the lights on the tree.

Michael followed and eased down beside her on the couch. Having dinner with Tammy felt right, as if they dined together every night. "What are your plans for Christmas?" He leaned back, hands laced behind his head.

She tucked one leg under her and turned to him. "I'm going to Joella and JD's house. This is the first Christmas their baby will be old enough to enjoy it." Tammy paused, plucking a small piece of lint off her jeans. "Unfortunately, my mom won't be with us. She passed away last year, and my father is in Europe. I miss them both terribly."

"I'm sorry to hear that. It must be hard."

A strand of hair fell onto her cheek, and she smoothed it back, a touch of mist gleaming in her eyes. "As a kid, I always thought my parents would be there forever. But now ... I didn't expect to lose her so soon." She cleared her throat. "What do you have planned?"

Tammy's loss reminded him how blessed he was. "I'll be going over to Mom and Dad's. Alexus, her husband, and the kids will be there too. And Darnell."

She smiled. "I think your parents did a good job teaching you determination. I admire anyone who can stick with the challenges of medical school and graduate." She traced a line on the couch fabric between them.

Not merely determination but spiritual guidance as well. "Thanks. It was a lifelong dream. But now, another goal monopolizes my thoughts. I want to build a specialty children's hospital in El Camino."

Like Alexus, Tammy's eyes brightened as he spoke of the plans. For twenty minutes, she didn't take her gaze from him as he outlined the project. Her sweet smile and occasional nods told him she believed in him.

When he finished, she clutched his hand. "If there's anything I can do to help, please let me know. Maybe organize a fundraiser or do research."

"I just may take you up on that. My dear, elderly secretary has unintentionally caused some problems, but I don't have the heart to come down on her too hard."

"The time when I brought the charity banquet tickets up to your office, she said you were married and moving your family away from El Camino. It was evident she believed it because she looked so sad."

"Oh, Iris." Michael tapped his forehead with the palm of his hand. "She totally missed what I said. She gets confused about things at times, but other than that, she's a great asset to the office."

Tammy peered at him. "That's another thing I love about you. You're gentle and care about people's feelings." Her gaze dropped to his lips, making his heart pound. No doubt she had more on her mind than listening to *I'm Dreaming of a White Christmas*. Maybe the kiss he'd given her at Starbucks.

He wanted to replay the moment. Before he thought, he slid his arm on the back of the couch around Tammy and leaned toward her.

Without a word, she moved closer to him, communicating her thoughts with a smile.

Michael drew her nearer and slowly captured her lips, the feel of her soft skin elevating his pulse.

Tammy wrapped her arms around him as she ran her fingers over his neck. Her lips traveled his chin to his ear, the warmth of her breath driving him to distraction.

The sweet moment became more urgent, his breath ragged. They were moving too fast. He needed to think about things before they went too far.

He used all that determination she said she liked about him to move away. His head hit the couch pillow as he leaned back a moment to slow his thoughts.

"Michael, don't stop," she whispered. The aroma of flowers was intoxicating as she breathed in his ear.

The look in her eyes. He knew ... he knew he shouldn't. But she was so near ... so warm and inviting. His body yearned for more. And he could tell she was willing. Something nagged at the back of his mind. Something he'd have to think about later.

"Hmm." She nibbled his ear.

The feel of her skin, the look in her eyes—but in God's sight, it wouldn't be right. "Tammy, we can't."

Lord, what am I doing? No longer able to resist, he became lost in her arms. He trailed his hand down her back and pulled her closer, his lips pressed against hers again.

He had only allowed himself to give into intimacy once, and then it was during his first year of medical school. He'd been taught to respect women, not place them in an awkward position. Yet now he couldn't turn back. Would God ignore them this once?

In a moment, Tammy rose from the couch and grasped his hand, gently tugging him toward the bedroom.

Michael followed thinking of nothing but his desire for her. As they neared the room, an inner Voice whispered. *This is wrong, Michael.* But he brushed the presence aside and walked hand-in-hand with her into the room where Tammy's queen-sized bed invited him.

*****

Tammy pressed her fingers to her cheek where Michael had just kissed her. The soft sound of the front door closing told her he'd gone. She glanced at her clock. 3:00 a.m.

Her mind roamed over every aspect of the evening beginning with the dinner they'd shared. Michael's prayer had surprised her. Was faith important to him like her sister's family? Or maybe saying a mealtime prayer was only a habit.

She rolled closer to the middle of the bed, smoothing her hand over the sheets, still warm where Michael had lain. The aroma of his woodsy after shave still clung to the pillow. She drew it into her lungs.

Her cheeks warmed. She didn't make a practice of inviting

guys to bed. Her parents had always impressed upon her their strict values. Though she'd rebelled in many ways, intimacy before marriage was one area she tried to honor—most of the time. What had possessed her? It was a good thing she had the necessary precautions on hand, left over from a health education class.

She whispered to his side of the bed, "Good night, Michael."

Then twinges of remorse nagged at her. Michael probably wouldn't have slept with her if she hadn't coaxed him. What if he believed as Joella? Had Tammy encouraged him to violate his religious principles? Yet he'd seemed more than willing.

Though being with Michael thrilled her, another thought gouged her. Tonight she'd shared how much she grieved over her mom and dad. In a strange way, had she sought intimacy to replace the affection she now missed from her father? She shuddered.

One thing was for sure. Tonight wasn't a one-night stand but more—much more. Though perhaps becoming intimate had been wrong, she was falling in love with Michael Clark.

*****

Michael slipped down beside his bed, shame filling his heart. He buried his face in the bedspread and murmured. "Lord, I'm sorry for the wrong I committed tonight. Please forgive me."

In the silence of his bedroom, he waited. Was sleeping with Tammy before marriage too sinful for God to pardon? After twenty minutes, the carpet seemed to dig into his knees, and he moved one leg to lift up.

Son, I forgave My servant David, and I also forgive you.

The words were more an impression than audibly spoken. Joy coursed through him. "Thank You, Lord."

Like David, there will be consequences.

Surely he hadn't perceived the message correctly. He covered his face with his hands and sank to the carpet. "Lord, in Your strength, I can face them."

Chapter Thirteen

Sounds of "Silent Night" played on Michael's car radio as he made the familiar drive to Mom and Dad's upscale Los Ranchos Grandes neighborhood. A large red and green Christmas wrapping bag filled to the brim with gifts for Mom, Dad, Alexus, her husband and kids, and Darnell rested in the backseat of his Mercedes. Christmas morning, a day he'd waited for all year long as a child, didn't bring the same joy today.

For a week now, he'd mulled over the guilt then the freeing forgiveness God offered. But consequences?

Though God had forgiven him, he still held disappointment in himself. He'd succumbed to his fleshy nature and disobeyed the Lord. No better than Samson in the Bible who became beguiled by Delilah, though ultimately Michael had to take full responsibility for his actions.

Mom made a big deal about inviting him to the candlelight service at her church last night, but he made up an excuse why he couldn't go. God had forgiven him, so why was it hard to forgive himself? The magic of the season had somehow vanished.

As if he'd taken a dip in the freezing cold waters of Big Lunas Creek, he shivered. What about Tammy's faith in God? He hadn't adequately considered her spiritual status before now—until he'd begun to fall in love with her.

When he pulled in front of Mom and Dad's house, he parked behind Darnell's silver Mercury and grasped the sturdy ribbon handle of the bag in the backseat. The aroma of a wood fire met his nose as he quivered against the chilly day.

The front door flew open and Toots with a wide grin and eyes gleaming, came bounding out. "Uncle Michael, what do you have for me?"

Michael put the bag down on the sidewalk and twirled Toots around. "Well, little man, you'll just have to wait until Grandma Clark says it's time for presents."

Picking up the bag again with one hand, he carried Toots inside the house and set him down in the entryway. "You can help me take out these packages and place them under the tree."

"Yea!" Toots began to carefully unpack Michael's bag.

After his nephew finished the job, Michael followed his nose to the kitchen where the aroma of pumpkin spice lured him. Mom stood over the oven checking the temperature gauge of a roasting turkey, and Alexus whipped fluffy mashed potatoes with an electric beater. "Where're those lazy guys? Aren't they helping?"

Mom turned from the stove and threw her arms around him. "Merry Christmas, son. I think they're all in the den watching some game. It's almost time for dinner anyway."

"Grandma Clark, when can we open presents?" Toots pulled on her apron.

"When we finish dinner." She grinned and patted him on the head. "You and your brother have been asking me that all morning."

After the family gathered once again in the spacious dining room, Alexus's husband said the blessing. Cranberry sauce and dressing, hot rolls, a relish tray, green beans casserole, and candied yams accompanied the turkey and mashed potatoes.

Michael chewed a bite of dressing and gravy then a wall plaque caught his attention. The words blazed into his thoughts, and he tried to look back at his plate, but finally he surrendered his attention to the message. "As far as the east is from the west, so far has He removed our sins from us." Psalm 103:12. Could it be true that God didn't remember what he and Tammy had done?

"Michael, you look like you're a thousand miles away, honey." Mom's voice broke through.

He coughed and glanced at his mother. "I'm sorry, what did you say?"

"Dad was wondering if you're dating anyone right now."

Darnell gave a raucous laugh. "He may not be dating her, but he's hanging out with a white nurse these days."

"Oh?" Mom took a bite of turkey.

Under the table, Michael found his foot tapping a steady rhythm. "She's just someone I met at the hospital." Though far from the truth, he couldn't tell his family what Tammy meant to him.

"Well, I think he's a fool. There are plenty of lovely black women out there," Darnell said.

"I don't see her as white or black. I enjoy spending time with her." Michael attempted to keep the agitation toward Darnell's comments out of his voice.

"I tend to agree with Darnell," Dad said. "Race is a hot-button issue these days. Why complicate your life bringing a white person into it? It could always lead to something more. How about any future children you may have? Would that create a hardship for them?"

"Dad, I'm not marrying her, for goodness' sake." Michael cringed. Though he'd given into lust. "But even if I were, mixed racial marriages are common today, including kids from those marriages."

"I think Dad and Darnell's concerns are misplaced. I'm more troubled by the young girls who get pregnant out of wedlock, regardless of their race," Mom said. "They're barely teenagers in some cases, incapable of being mothers. So many come from homes that have lost their moral compass." She directed her gaze at Michael again. "The most important thing is that any girl you date, whether she's black or white, holds to the Christian faith."

Michael opened his mouth to answer but in reality, what could he say? Once again, the notion hit. He had no idea whether Tammy was a Christian.

"You still haven't told us her name," Darnell chided.

Sweat rolled down Michael's neck. Christmas dinner wasn't working out like he'd anticipated. "Tammy Crawford," he said against his better judgment. "Her sister is married to El Camino's prominent CPA, JD Neilson." Maybe that would impress them.

Alexus, sitting next to him, squeezed his hand. "Hey, you guys, leave Michael alone. You're grilling him. He's only dating her, nothing more."

Michael released the breath he'd held. He could count on his sister to stand up for him.

"I agree," Mom said. "These two grandbabies have waited long enough. Everyone finish your meal, and we'll move into the living room to open presents."

Eating the rest of the food on his plate was a chore, but Mom would notice if Michael didn't finish it.

Finally he rose from the table when the others began to help pile the dishes in the sink. He grabbed a handful, took them to the kitchen, then followed the rest as they sat down around the tree.

A nudge to his ribs demanded his attention. Darnell glared at him. "I'm telling you, you're an idiot if you allow that relationship to go far."

Cold pinpricks poked Michael's spine. Little did Darnell know, it was too late.

*****

The garage door glided up after Michael pushed the button on the remote. He parked and retrieved his large bundle of gifts from the back seat. Christmas with children was always unpredictable, but he couldn't blame his unease on the kids. Alexus's sons were well behaved, nice little boys. Maybe someday he'd have a child, and if he did, he wanted him to be like Toots and Jeremy.

How had Tammy spent the day? That thought bubbled up from the hundreds of others in his head and in his heart. With each passing week, his affection for her deepened, and he found himself thinking about her at every idle moment. Though he'd never fallen in love before, when her beautiful face popped into his mind, he became more convinced he had.

But two major obstacles stood in the way: his family and not knowing if Tammy loved the Lord. He never anticipated getting to this point in his life with these issues at stake.

Michael set the packages in the living room and flopped down on the couch. No matter what, Mom, Dad, Darnell, and Alexus were still his family, and he appreciated them.

Feeling vulnerable after his brother's scrutiny, he allowed himself to verbalize the truth. "Lord, I may have fallen in love with an unbeliever."

He sat up straight on the couch. Why had he spoken the words and what were the answers? Maybe if he had more time with Tammy, he could find out where she stood and share his faith with her.

This morning's paper had featured a picture on the front page of the downtown park where they'd jogged. A sixty-foot Christmas cedar with more than eighty thousand lights illuminated the area. He'd ask her to go with him tomorrow night and grab hot chocolate later at one of the coffee bars nearby. Perhaps tell her he regretted the night when they fell into bed. He would be a better example next time.

*****

Tammy savored the aroma of the steaming mug of creamy hot chocolate topped with marshmallows. The warmth traveled down her chest as she gazed out the window of the corner coffee shop. The tree lights twinkled from the park with hues of red, green, silver, gold, and white on the sixty-foot cedar. Bringing her attention back to the man sharing the high-topped table, she lifted her gaze to him.

Michael's focus appeared to be fixed on her face, as if searching for an answer. Was he questioning their romance? She slid her fingers over his. "The lights were enchanting. Thanks for asking me to share them with you."

He squeezed her hand and leaned back in his chair, his expression more relaxed. After a sip of chocolate, he gazed at her again. "Tammy, I need to ask you—"

"Joy to the world, the Lord has come." A group of carolers with red noses and bright faces stepped inside the cafe. "Let earth receive her king."

"Now, if we weren't in a seasonal mood, we are now." Tammy giggled.

Michael scratched the back of his neck and cast his gaze toward them. "I think you're right."

After several more songs, the boisterous group shouted, "Merry Christmas. The Lord has come," and walked out of the cafe.

After he and Tammy drained their mugs, Michael pitched a

couple of bills on the table and smiled. "Are you ready? We can walk through the park one more time and look at the tree."

Tammy nodded, stepped down from the chair, and buttoned up her down jacket. "Ready."

As they strolled along the sidewalk to Michael's car on the other side of the park, he smiled and grasped her hand.

A middle-age couple, sauntering past them stared then whispered to each other. A quiver did battle with the hot chocolate in her stomach. Hadn't they ever seen a black man holding a white woman's hand? Ridiculous.

She glanced up at Michael to observe his reaction.

He seemed to focus on the concrete path, apparently lost in thought.

Then she remembered when the carolers came into the coffee shop. "What were you going to say earlier?"

He stared at her a minute. "I wanted to ask you... I think ... Oh, it's all right. We can talk about it later. But tell me you'll go with me to a concert at North California U right after the first of the year. The Masters of Hawaiian Music will be performing their first concert then.

Her lips parted in a grin, and she couldn't wipe away the smile that she knew filled her face. "I'd love to." Whatever bothered Michael before no longer seemed to worry him now.

WHAT GOD KNEW

Chapter Fourteen

Michael grasped Tammy's hand as they strolled from the events center on the NCU campus. Every minute with her felt comfortable and fun. But something continued to pester him—her standing with the Lord. All his life he'd learned about not forming serious relationships with unbelievers. At the park downtown before New Year's, he'd started to ask her about her faith but changed his mind. The subject needed to come up naturally. Instead he turned his thoughts to the riveting, one-of-a-kind performance they'd just witnessed. "I'm not sure about you, but I'm ready to wiggle my toes in the beach at Waikiki." Two hours of Polynesian music had whisked him away to the sandy shores.

Tammy lifted her eyes, now the color of the Hawaiian Palm tree. "I'd love to go to the island one day. Especially if you were with me."

Her words tempted him to dream of walking the balmy beaches, listening to the bubbly music of the ukulele, and sniffing the aroma of wild ginger and plumeria. The state was known as the paradise of the Pacific for a reason.

But the two of them taking a trip together now? Only if they were man and wife.

Clicking the locks on his Mercedes, he helped Tammy in the passenger side, trying to avoid glancing at her shapely legs and thighs as she scooted in. Revving up the engine, he pulled out of the parking lot and onto the street that took them off campus.

Almond Lane, a road through a less populated part of El

Camino, led north from campus to Tammy's neighborhood. "This isn't Hawaii, but this route gives more of a country feel than the interstate."

Tammy ran her hand down his shoulder. "I suppose being anywhere with you makes me happy, Michael."

In the car's enclosed interior, the fragrance of jasmine and sandalwood captivated him again. The same scent that had filled his senses the night he'd been with her—now begging to cripple his resolve.

Arriving in front of Tammy's apartment building, he parked and walked around to the passenger side. After trekking up the stairs to her second-floor apartment, they paused at her door.

She pulled out her keys, opened the lock, then turned to him. "Come in for a while—for coffee." Her gleaming green eyes twinkled as her gaze lingered on him.

He leaned down to kiss Tammy's lips then whispered. "There's something I need to say—the other night when we were together ... when I stayed with you ..." He cleared his throat. "Tammy, I'm a Christian, and I can't fall into intimacy again. It's not ... not pleasing to God."

"I thought maybe you were." She cast her gaze to her folded hands. "I need to tell you I'm sorry for encouraging you. It was wrong."

Tammy's apology eased his doubts a little. It took a lot of courage for her to say the words. "It was as much my doing as yours. I should've lived up to my moral standards."

"As a girl, I was raised with those same standards." She gazed at the wall over his shoulder. "This is not an excuse, but I allowed myself to be caught up in the moment that night."

He took her hands and pressed them to his chest. "I need to ask you. How do you feel about God? I mean are you a follower of the Messiah Jesus Christ?"

Pink filled her cheeks. "I'd like to tell you I am, but I can't. All my life my family has told me about their faith and what they believe. I respect them—and you—for your point of view. Everyone is entitled to their way of thinking, but somehow I can't bring myself to accept that there's a big man upstairs directing everything I do. I think it's better to admit that than fake it."

"I admire you for your truthfulness." As if a rock had fallen and crushed his dreams, he faced reality. By her own words, Tammy wasn't a believer. But maybe if he gave it time, she would eventually accept the faith. Pushing it down her throat certainly wouldn't work. *Lord, help me to be a good example to her.* "Thank you for being honest. I care a lot about you, Tammy Crawford."

"And thank you for the evening."

After another kiss, he took the stairs to the entrance of the building and to his car on the street. He'd discovered what he needed to know, but would Tammy ever give her heart to the Lord? They had no future if she didn't.

*****

The aroma of antiseptic and detergent filled Tammy's nose as she neared Mr. Tolbert's room. At eighty-five years of age, the courageous man fought congestive heart failure. Based on stats of other cases like his, she doubted he'd survive much longer, but she wanted to make his stay at the hospital as comfortable as possible.

She sighed and allowed her mind to switch from her patient to Michael, who had occupied her thoughts most of her free time since they went out last week. Though the new year had come, there hadn't been much time to see each other. Maybe it was for the best. She didn't want to admit it, but she desired that closeness with Michael again. Yet if they were alone in her apartment, she didn't want to tempt him—or herself.

Though her motives to avoid intimacy weren't based on religion like Michael's, she still remembered the standards her parents required of her and Joella. Sure society said it was okay, but her upbringing had become deeply ingrained.

As if cold water dribbled down her back, she gasped. What if Michael was like Joella? What if he started preaching at her, trying to get her to believe as he did?

Switching her attention back to work, Tammy braced as she entered Mr. Tolbert's room, afraid to observe his deteriorating condition. Taking his blood pressure and other vitals would be telling. She made a mental note not to forget to look for swelling in his lower extremities and to evaluate his level of comfort and awareness. Recording the information on his chart daily was imperative and a practice she prided herself in doing. Her patients deserved quality care.

Mr. Tolbert lay in the bed, his eyes closed.

Tammy watched his chest rising and falling in irregular movements, the result of shallow breathing. "Hello, Mr. Tolbert," she whispered.

He slowly opened his eyes. "Hello, dear. I — " He broke into a spasm of coughing fits then turned to her again.

The kindly patient she'd gotten to know the last two weeks barely lifted the corners of his mouth, as if a smile took all his effort. "I'm so glad you came into see me. Do you have time to sit by my side a moment?" He lifted a thin hand, spotted by age marks.

Tammy's heart filled with compassion for the elderly patient, one of the reasons she'd chosen geriatrics. She loved aging people with their stories of long ago and the simplicity of yesteryear. "Of course, sir." She slipped down into the bedside chair and grasped his cool hand.

With watery blue eyes that spoke of years of life's experiences behind him, he squeezed her hand. "I miss my old fishin' hole more than I can say." He paused for another coughing spell. "If I could take my pole and go down to the pond near my house one more time, I'd be grateful. When my son was young, he used to go along, too." The gentleman closed his eyes a moment and gasped for breath.

Tammy ran her hand over his forehead and neck. His skin was cool as she'd suspected.

Mr. Tolbert opened his eyes again. "Yep. My boy grew up to be a successful business man, but I can still see him as a little tike with bright blue eyes watching the frogs jumping into the old pond." He turned his head on the pillow to look at Tammy. "I miss those days more than anything else now. I suppose I won't ever get back to fishin' again." A trickle of moisture rolled down his cheek.

Words evaded her. The man was right. He neared death and would never go out with a pole and a bucket of worms again, but what could she say? She couldn't offer him hope. She could only keep him comfortable.

A wet, noisy cough overcame Mr. Tolbert once more. He gave Tammy another weak smile and closed his eyes. "I think I'll take a little nap now."

Tammy squeezed his hand again and sat a few more minutes until his breathing became more rhythmic. She quietly rose from the chair, checked the IV delivering the antibiotics to his body, and tiptoed out of the room.

Walking down the hall back to the nurses' station, she glanced at her watch. Time to leave for the day. She gathered up her purse and coat from her locker, trying to shake the empty void in her chest. Each step toward the elevator was an effort. Mr. Tolbert's health must've bothered her more than she'd realized, yet the last couple of days she'd dragged through her shifts, her energy depleted. Exhaustion hadn't overwhelmed her like this since nursing school during finals week.

Stepping into the elevator, she touched the *down* button then her cell phone rang. Michael. "Hey, Dr. Clark."

"I'm sorry this is last minute. Would you have dinner with me?"

The elevator door slid open, and Tammy got off at the ground floor. "I would love it, but I had a rough day. One of my patients really got to me. He told me how his poor health kept him from the things he loves to do, like fishing. I felt so sorry for the guy."

"I'm sorry. One of the negatives of our profession is seeing people suffer."

"True, and now I can barely drag myself home. I think I'm coming down with something." She staggered out through the front door to the employee's parking lot.

"I'd recommend you get a checkup soon."

"I'd like to have an appointment with a good-looking pediatrician I know, but I suppose I should see my internist."

He laughed. "The pediatrician might not be able to think straight, and he'd misdiagnosis you."

Though her laugh was weak, Tammy found a smile on her face. "I'm heading home now."

"Okay," he whispered. "Take care of yourself. I miss you."

Though having dinner with Michael thrilled her, Tammy could only think of one thing. Getting home to take a long, relaxing bath.

*****

The next afternoon, Tammy's normal energy level hadn't

returned. Though she loved caring for her patients, it had taken every last ounce of effort to perform her job. If her strength didn't pick up soon, she'd prescribe a multivitamin for herself or attempt to eat more regular meals. A doctor's exam to check her thyroid and blood cell count would be another option.

With weary steps, Tammy trudged down the hall toward the night nurse who scanned her computer screen. "See you tomorrow, Beth." She lifted a heavy hand and waved at her colleague.

"Oh, Tammy." Beth rose from her seat behind the desk. "Do you have a moment?"

Though her body screamed to go home and take a nap, Tammy stopped. "Sure." She turned toward the unassuming woman with ash blonde hair and copper highlights approaching in the hall near the employee's lockers.

Beth lowered her voice. "I need to ask you a question. Last night when I checked on Mr. Tolbert, I noticed that you hadn't made any entries on his chart. Just wondering if you overlooked it."

Though exhausted, defiance shot through her. A first year RN had accused her of not doing her job. "Of course, I recorded it. You merely overlooked it."

Beth's face reddened. "I … I checked his chart and didn't see anything."

"Well, go check it again." What happened to her patience? She stormed into the employees' room, grabbed her coat and purse, and stomped to the elevators, adrenalin driving her.

After twenty minutes, Tammy dragged her tired body into her apartment and collapsed onto the couch. She leaned back and closed her eyes. Beth's horrified face popped into her memory.

As if blasted with a hot wind, Tammy opened her eyes. Thoughts of her visit with Mr. Tolbert last night slunk through her memory. She'd sat by his bed, empathy for the man almost evoking tears. When he'd dropped off to sleep, she'd checked his IV and walked out of the room.

A cold sweat covered her body. Beth was right. Tammy hadn't recorded his vitals or other symptoms. Only one thing to do—make a late-entry tomorrow.

She fingered her cell phone and punched in the phone number for the geriatric ward. Though it shamed her, she could only do one thing: apologize.

"Ms. Logan."

"Beth, this is Tammy. I need to tell you I'm sorry. You're right. I forgot to make the entry. No excuse but I didn't feel well tonight and lost it."

"Oh, Tammy. Thank you so much for calling. I understand. I hope you get a good-night's rest and are doing better tomorrow."

"Thanks." Barely dragging herself in the bathroom to get ready for bed, Tammy determined she'd see her internist as soon as possible.

*****

After a week, Tammy didn't feel any better. She tugged on her pajamas and switched the laptop on. Seeing the doctor hadn't fit in her schedule yet, but she had to stop procrastinating. The only bright spot was facing Beth with a clear conscience after asking for her pardon.

She rubbed her sour stomach and glanced at the computer screen, trying to ignore her growing suspicions. Only one last grant to apply for tonight—The American Association of Nurse Practitioners. She'd already completed the one for The American College of Nurse Practitioners and several government sponsored opportunities in November. Hopefully she'd hear from one of them.

After an hour, she finished the application and clicked *send*. Once again, the notion encouraged her. Getting a Nurse Practitioner certification would allow her to rise higher in her profession and provide better pay.

Stretching didn't loosen her stiff neck and arms as her thoughts turned to Michael. Though most days lately she'd only had enough power to hobble home, she still longed to spend time with him. Hopefully, there'd be an opportunity soon.

Chapter Fifteen

Michael hung up the office phone, only slightly encouraged since Mr. Jamison said he regretted the confusion before he went to Europe and would consider financial backing again. But he wouldn't be in a position to act for a while.

With rounds completed, Michael could think about going home in the next few minutes—and he could see if Tammy might feel like going to dinner with him. Lately he'd only called at the last minute, not sure of how she'd feel each day. If he were to guess, Tammy didn't eat a proper diet and didn't get the nutrition she needed. Perhaps she suffered from anemia.

He pulled out his cell and punched her speed dial number.

"Hey, Michael." The same weak voice answered.

"Have you seen a doc yet? I'm starting to get worried about you."

"Honestly, I've been putting it off. I suppose if something is wrong, I'm not sure if I want to know." She gave a soft chuckle.

"Tammy Crawford, if I have to make an appointment for you and escort you there, I will." He tossed a wadded piece of paper in the garbage pail and missed. "If you don't feel like having dinner tonight, at least meet me for lunch tomorrow."

"I'd like to."

"See you then. Get some rest tonight."

A soft chuckle met his ear. "I will."

Michael turned his attention back to his file with the hospital plans. He carefully placed the newly printed copies of the original information that had been lost—his web search on the advantages and disadvantages of building versus buying an existing building. Then the lists of available structures in the area, El Camino's best commercial contractors, and the list of potential board members who'd all agreed to come to an exploratory meeting. This time he'd keep the file in his briefcase without fail.

The date on the desk calendar was circled. The day he'd scheduled the conference room. Iris assured him she wouldn't forget to reserve it.

The hospital directory still lay open to Mr. Reynolds' entry and phone number. One positive step—the hospital administrator had given him a stamp of approval to pursue construction of a pediatric hospital, supporting him one hundred percent. El Camino County needed a specialty facility, and it would in no way compete with El Camino General.

He carefully deposited the file in his briefcase and snapped it shut as his cell phone rang. Maybe Tammy felt better and could go to dinner after all.

Michael shook his head. The caller ID said Darnell. "Hi, bro. How's it going?"

"Hey. I haven't talked to you for a while. How about meeting me at the Almond Tree Bar and Grill for a drink?" His brother's slurred words sounded like he'd been there an hour or so.

"You know I don't drink," Michael said.

"That's okay. You can get some appetizers or something. Come on down." Sounds of a noisy crowd met his ear.

Darnell was right. They hadn't seen each other in a few weeks, and he was family. A break would do him good, too. "Okay, see you soon. I'm leaving now."

After a twenty minute drive to the south side of the college campus, Michael pulled up in front of the English Pub-style bar that appealed to the university crowd.

Thoughts of Darnell's behavior the night he took Tammy to Giorgio's still bothered him, but he'd ignore them tonight. He opened the stained-glass doors and spotted his brother at a small table toward one end of the room which was filled with a twenties' crowd.

Darnell waved and downed the last of the amber beverage in his pilsner glass. He motioned to the waitress. "Give me another one of these. And whatever my brother wants."

"I'll have a soda, thanks." Michael slid into the Windsor chair opposite him.

The waitress nodded and turned toward an ornate, hand-carved wooden bar on the other side of the room.

"Glad you could make it. We haven't seen each other since Christmas. How are you doing?"

The waitress returned, and Michael thanked her for the soda. "I'm fine. How are things with you?"

"Same old stuff I'm always doing." Darnell tipped back his new drink. "There are a lot of needy folks in the world." He sat the glass down on the table. "Ever wonder why most of them are black?"

"No. I don't need to wonder. Our culture has been decimated by single-parent families and a lack of education." He straightened in his seat when Darnell started to raise his hand in protest. "No, let me finish. I listen to you run off about your convictions, and I haven't said much in deference to Mom and Dad, but now that you've started the conversation and we're alone, I want to take part in it. Have my say."

Darnell lifted a brow but remained silent.

"Our culture isn't the only one suffering from poverty, but I think you've been so focused on making your hypothesis fit your convictions, you've forgotten that your non-profit serves people regardless of their color. I'd hate to think that your prejudice has harmed someone who is not of our color, someone who needs help because of the circumstances they've found themselves in. Look around you, *bro*. Those issues Mom talks about—they effect more than our race." Michael took a breath.

"Are you still dating that white girl, or have you come to your senses?" Obviously, his brother's mind was closed to the truth, and he wanted to change the subject.

"It's really none of your business, Darnell, but we're going to have lunch."

"I'll tell you why it's my business. You're a successful doctor." Darnell squinted and lowered his voice. "That's the only reason a white woman would think about dating you."

Michael tensed, waiting for the next round of reprimands.

"I'm going to lay it out for you." His brother shook a finger in his face. "Look at all the white women hanging on the professional athletes and entertainers. It's the same thing with you."

"You're out of your mind. That's not the way it is with Tammy and me." He winced. Too much information for Darnell to know.

"Look, I care about you." Darnell folded hands on the table and leaned nearer. "You're my brother. Just listen to me." He fixed his focus on Michael's face. "Dating a white girl weakens the community as a whole. Haven't you noticed the gaping financial disparities between them and us in general? Systematic oppression and targeted violence have only widened the gap. Who do you think is responsible? Don't you get it, brother? Whites have suppressed our people far too long."

Michael shook his head. "You didn't listen to a thing I said. You're taking up someone else's talking points. These days, with the economy the way it is, the only oppression comes from the lack of a job, the lack of an education, and the lack of a relationship with God. That's not exclusive to African-Americans. I'll admit that cultural differences and oppression of African-Americans existed in the past and still exist in isolated areas of the country today, but as a whole, things have changed. Overall people are responsible for their own lives. God controls mine and provides my needs. He has placed people like you in the paths of the needy to be a conduit of His goodness. I don't want to talk this racist rhetoric with you again."

"You've been listening to Mom too long. Get real. Until we gain power, we'll have no peace. Do you want to connect with a white person who represents injustices toward our people?"

Michael stared at his brother. Somewhere along the line, Darnell had been radicalized. Yet nothing could bankrupt Michael's faith in the Lord. "You never talked like this when we were teenagers."

"That's right." Darnell firmed his lips then he blared. "My thinking has changed. Mom lives in a dream world filled with religious myths, and though Dad doesn't encourage mixed racial connections, he never really gives a lot of thought to the subject. In the past, he was always too busy fighting wars to form a valid opinion."

"Fighting wars for a country that gave him the opportunity to make something of himself, Darnell. Our dad is a general. He took advantage of the freedom in our country to better himself and to make a great life for his family. He stayed with his wife; he raised his kids, and now, he's worshipping the Lord. Those are all the things I told you are missing from many other cultures in America, not just ours." Again, he took a deep breath. "So, tell me what changed your thinking?"

"You're wrong. I was real lucky. My university days finally opened my eyes, and the public policy classes provided plenty of information on the subject. A prime example is the stats that show the majority of whites don't vote for black candidates. I learned the truth then, and I want you to understand as well."

The cold bubbly liquid refreshed Michael as he sipped on his drink. He didn't hold his brother's conclusions, but he would let Darnell have his say. His brother held strong convictions. There were undoubtedly many others in the black community who felt the same.

Not that he wanted this to influence things with Tammy. Yet connecting with her would create more complications than with a woman of his race. Were they capable of facing the challenges? And would Tammy commit her life to the Savior?

*****

As Tammy stepped out of the elevator, she spotted Michael waiting in front of the cafeteria.

His face lit with a grin that stretched across his lips. "How are you today?"

"Better, thanks." So far this morning, the fatigue that hung over her for days hadn't gripped her as usual.

He squeezed her hand. "I'm so glad."

After filling their trays in the cafeteria line, Tammy followed Michael to a table for two near the window. Aware of his custom, she waited while he prayed.

After he took a sip of iced tea, he focused on her. "So tell me, really, how do you feel? Maybe you should get checked for anemia."

Michael's concern warmed her heart, but the nagging suspicion that had remained with her for days brought distraction. She propelled the notion to the farthest corner of her mind. If she refused to believe, maybe it wouldn't be true. "I think I'm better. Really, Michael, I probably wasn't eating properly. I'm trying to change that." She looked down at her plate of baked chicken, mashed potatoes, green beans, and apple pie and laughed. "This meal is a start."

Michael bit off a piece of his roast beef sandwich and chewed. "Just promise me, if you feel worse, you'll see your internist."

"I will." If her symptoms meant anything, she wouldn't need an internist. She'd be seeking out an obstetrician.

*****

After Michael's lunch with Tammy three days ago, he considered asking her again today, but the NICU kept him busy without a break.

The thirty-week infant lay in the incubator. Michael carefully removed the tiny earphones he'd placed in the baby's ear canal earlier and the miniature sensors taped to the baby's head.

Glancing at the audio screener, he frowned. Anxiety filled him as he feared the diagnosis he didn't want to make. The child was likely deaf.

His next step would be to talk to the parents and then with Dr. Valentine for a second opinion. Reporting bad news to worried new parents was one of the worst aspects of his job, but a necessity.

Michael recorded his findings on the infant's chart, headed to the elevator, and pressed *down* for labor and delivery. After checking with the nurse on duty, he made the trek along the hall to the mother's private room. Stopping at the entrance, he took a deep breath and tapped on the door then walked in.

A thirty-something man sat in a chair beside a smiling blonde lying in the bed.

"Mr. and Mrs. Kinsey, I'm Dr. Clark, one of the neonatal specialists from the NIC unit. May I speak with you a moment?"

Mr. Kinsey rose. "Yes, please come in."

"I performed a thorough examination of your baby. Everything looks fine except in one area."

Mrs. Kinsey's drew a hand to her mouth, and Mr. Kinsey firmed his jaw, staring at Michael.

"Preemie babies are at risk for a number of health concerns including hearing loss. I performed an Otoacoustic Emissions test or an OAE on your baby. I'm sorry to report that I have reason to believe he's likely hearing impaired and possibly deaf."

Tears formed in Mrs. Kinsey's eyes, her smile vanishing. "Are you sure, Doctor?"

"Dr. Jeff Valentine, one of the other specialists on the team, will offer a second opinion and administer a different test, the Auditory Brainstem Response or ABR. I assure you, both tests are safe and comfortable for the baby."

Mr. Kinsey bent over the bed toward his wife who buried her face in his arms weeping. He looked up at Michael, his voice breaking. "We're stunned. We never expected something like that."

As if the child were his own, he empathized with the parents. He strode toward the bed and placed a hand on Mr. Kinsey's shoulder. "I'm sorry." Watching a new mother shed tears was never easy. In this case, the thought of the little child living his life never hearing a musical performance or falling rain or a bird's song brought deep regret.

The brokenhearted father nodded, brushing a tear from his cheek, and turned back to his wife.

"There are many services and agencies to assist the hearing impaired. You have options. I'd like to encourage you with that." Michael stepped quietly out of the room and took the elevator to the fourth floor and the main doctors' lounge. A cup of coffee would help settle the tension.

After filling a mug with hot liquid, he strolled to the long glass window, looking out at the busy sidewalk below. El Camino citizens scurried along, unaware that parents of a premature baby were grieving.

"Hi, Michael."

Tammy. Michael's outlook brightened a little. He slowly turned from the window to face the perky young nurse. No doubt she could read the concern on his face.

A gentle smile lifted the corners of her mouth, compassion radiating from her eyes. She neared him and laid her hand on his arm. "Is everything okay?"

He peered into her twinkling green eyes. "Doctors train for years with the hope of helping patients get better. At times, when there are no more human options, we have to give those we're treating over to God." Michael hadn't planned to speak of the Lord right now, but he was grateful for the opportunity to talk about his faith to Tammy. Surprisingly, the words seemed to be God's own special message for him. He thanked the Savior for the privilege of laying before Him the deaf newborn.

Tammy's face was filled with sympathy as she rubbed his arm. "I've got a thirty-minute break right now. Would you like to take a walk in the hospital gardens? It might help."

*****

Strolling down the flagstone path through leafless live oaks and sugar maples settled Michael. He turned to Tammy beside him and grasped her hand. Her support right now bolstered his frame of mind.

"Let's sit here for a few minutes." Tammy pointed to a wooden shelter with benches under a shingle roof.

He eased down beside her in the deserted gazebo, and she squeezed his hand. "What you said earlier—about giving your patient to God—is that something people in your church say when they run out of other alternatives?"

Michael gazed at her a moment, searching her face. Her question struck him as almost childlike. "In this world, we all arrive at the limit of our abilities. In geriatrics, elderly people die despite the excellent care they receive. Some disorders are inevitable and incurable regardless of the knowledge we in the medical field have acquired. We come to the end of ourselves and then find God on the other side."

"God, hmm. This is a complex question, but what is the difference between God and religion?" Tammy furrowed her brow. "I've always thought religious people were weak and needed to believe in God as sort of a crutch."

Michael chuckled. "I'm not a theologian, but there's one great difference that I know of. God is the Creator of all things—this earth, mankind, and the entire universe. Religion is man's feeble efforts to reach God—practices and rituals we believe necessary to connect with Him." He took a breath. "There's nothing we can do to work our way to God. But He, in His grace, offered a Way for mankind to know Him. Not by any religious practices, but through a relationship."

"Is that where Jesus comes in?"

"Exactly. God came to earth in the form of a man to offer salvation to any who ask."

"You've given me so much to think about. When Joella talks about religion, I mean about Jesus, she makes me feel like I'm not good enough."

"I don't know your sister well, but I can almost guarantee her message is rooted in love. Tammy, Jesus didn't come into the world to condemn us but to save us." Words began to clog in his throat as he realized God had provided this opportunity to talk about Him to Tammy. Without another word, he stood, offering her a hand up.

As naturally as relaxing in his easy chair, she fell into his embrace, wrapping her arms tightly around him.

The warmth of Tammy's body and her nearness soothed like a balmy shower. He shut his eyes and clung to her. Tammy in his arms, a missing piece in his life. *But Lord, will she give her heart to the Savior?*

*****

Michael set his cup of coffee down and looked at Jeff. "This spot okay?"

"Sure." Jeff Valentine took the seat across from him at the small table. He sipped his coffee gazing intently at Michael. "I'm afraid I can only confirm your findings. The baby has complete hearing loss."

Michael nodded. The announcement came as no surprise.

His friend looked down at his coffee cup and up to him. "Would you like for me to meet with the parents to confirm the results?"

"Yeah, thanks." Michael stirred the cream into the coffee, watching it swirl then blend into the steaming liquid.

"Will do, buddy." Jeff grinned. "Hey, how many years have we known each other? I can tell something is on your mind. Care to tell me?"

Jeff wasn't supposed to be so perceptive, yet they'd been

friends, both professionally and personally. "Oh, nothing, really. Just the usual."

"The usual Dr. Clark is enthusiastic and readily interacts with others. If I didn't know better, I'd say you've built a towering wall around yourself."

Michael laughed. "I thought you practiced pediatrics, not psychology."

"What's going on, buddy? I'm a good listener."

Michael opened his mouth to deny Jeff's comments but shrugged. "Okay, if you must know, it's about a woman."

"I figured as much."

Though an African-American, Jeff probably wouldn't think like Darnell. Maybe talking to him about Tammy wouldn't hurt. "There's a nurse here at the hospital. I think I'm falling for her." He cracked his knuckles.

"That doesn't sound like a problem to me."

"Yeah, but there's something I didn't tell you. She's white."

"Hmm." Jeff scratched his chin.

Michael's stomach knotted. Jeff was going to give him a kinder version of Darnell's message.

"Hey, if you're in love with her, go for it." Jeff grinned. "These days, mixed marriages are more prevalent than fifty years ago."

Not the words he'd expected. "Thanks."

"You got it." Jeff glanced at his watch. "I need to get going. Let's meet for coffee again."

Michael nodded and watched his friend amble out of the cafeteria. Though Jeff supported him, two facts still remained: his brother didn't approve of Tammy at all, and his father would tolerate her at best. Michael could neither deny the racial tension their association would create nor Tammy's spiritual views. He shook his head. *Lord, show me what to do.*

WHAT GOD KNEW

Chapter Sixteen

Tammy stumbled out of the bathroom gripping the home pregnancy tester in her fist. How could the results on one small device threaten to change her life forever? And how ironic was it? Michael—the first guy she'd been with since college and then only once.

Until now she hadn't wanted to give into her suspicions but could no longer ignore the new symptoms of nausea and a tender chest. For weeks, she'd hoped the evidence was merely in her mind, but now she knew it wasn't. Not a Valentine's gift she would've asked for, especially not on a Saturday morning off.

Still unwilling to allow the ramifications to sink in, she shook her head. Maybe the test was wrong. She'd try it again in a day or two. But she knew the truth. Home tests were ninety-nine percent accurate.

Incredible. The measure they'd taken hadn't worked. The small percentage rate of failure had prevailed.

She paced her living room, trying to absorb the information. If truly pregnant, a decision loomed, and she needed to face facts. Marriage and a baby had never been a part of her life plan. But more than that, other factors plagued her.

What were her choices? Raising a baby by herself. Or—marry Michael. But would their union work? His brother would no doubt object, and what about the rest of his family?

She plopped down on the couch, drawing her legs to her chest. In a meager attempt to comfort herself, she hugged her knees and closed her eyes. How did she feel about marriage to Michael? If she were honest, it was a bit late to think about that. She'd placed herself in a vulnerable position. Not a smart move for a career woman. She loved Michael, but at the same time wanted to pursue her profession.

But what about Michael's feelings? He knew she didn't believe as he did. He might not want to marry her because of that. But she couldn't fake a worldview she didn't embrace.

A wave of nausea sent her dashing for the bathroom. When the retching subsided, she sat on the edge of the tub, gasping for air. More bothersome than morning sickness, the next thought smacked her in the center of her stomach. There was another alternative—get rid of the fetus. The solution seemed simple and afterward they could both go on with their lives as if nothing happened.

But abortion? She hadn't really thought about her beliefs as she'd never needed to before. If she did rid herself of the problem, Michael would never have to know. Nor anyone at the hospital or her sister.

Yet in fairness, she needed to tell him. As a Christian, he'd probably try to talk her out of it. It was her body, though, and she had the right to decide.

Slowly, she stumbled back into the living room and located her purse. Reaching in, she retrieved her cell phone. She'd ask Michael to drop by later in the day. Her stomach clenched, from nerves or her queasiness, she couldn't be sure. When his voice mail completed the announcement, she cleared her throat. "Michael, would you please drop by my place later when you get a chance. I need to talk to you."

*****

Michael pressed his finger on the doorbell at Tammy's apartment. He tried to ignore the turmoil building in his gut as he waited. Her voice on the other end of the phone message sounded as if she'd received less than pleasant news. Obviously something bothered her.

Perhaps she'd gone to the internist, and things didn't look good. Could she have cancer? He gritted his teeth not knowing what to expect or why she wanted to talk to him. He only knew he cared about her deeply and would stand by her no matter how sick she was. He took a shallow breath of air.

A pale-faced Tammy opened the door and stepped back for him to enter. His fears were confirmed. Tammy must be seriously ill.

"Sit down, Michael. There's something we have to talk about." She pointed to the couch.

He dropped down beside her on the comfy sofa where he'd sat the night of the Mexican dinner. The piece of furniture now felt like a hard bench. He turned to face the thin woman with dark circles under her eyes. "I need for you to know. No matter how poor your health, I'm here for you." He reached for her hand. "I'll pray every day, and we'll get you the best medical care."

Tammy's eyes widened as if she didn't believe him. "That's thoughtful, but I'm afraid medical science—or anything else isn't going to help." She pulled her hand from his and wrapped it around her middle. "Only time."

Had he heard correctly? "What are you saying?"

She jumped from the couch and paced the floor. Her creamy white face bleached even paler. She stood as still as a child playing a game of "Hide and Seek" then slowly turned to him.

"Something's terribly wrong. Tell me what it is. I care about you and everything that concerns you."

For a moment, her features softened, as if his words brought comfort, then a hardened mask seemed to transform her face again in self determination. "I've got to tell you something, and I don't know any other way to say it. This isn't easy, and it's nothing I expected."

The worse possible scenario—the gravest illness he could fathom hovered in his mind. "Is it cancer?"

She gulped a breath. "No, Michael. Nothing like that." She paused, clearing her throat then lifted her gaze to him. "I'm afraid I'm pregnant."

Pregnant? The last thing he thought she'd say. "But how? We … Are you sure?"

She shook her head. "I took a home pregnancy test. I still don't understand how it could've happened, but it did."

He sat motionless, stunned by the news. Her symptoms of

fatigue had nothing to do with a disease or disorder but the early stages of pregnancy. The verse from the Word echoed in his mind. *We reap what we sow.* The results of what he'd done made impact with his brain. Christians weren't immune to God's laws. Now he fully understood the words—*like David, there will be consequences.*

"From the look on your face, I can see that you feel as trapped as I do at the moment." Tammy dotted a tissue under her eyes. "I want to make it plain—we have options. One is abortion."

"No, Tammy." *Dear Lord, help me explain this.* "I've dedicated my career to saving innocent little children. How could I ever take the life of a child—especially my own?" He stood and paced the room. "Our baby isn't just an embryo. Tammy, he or she is a real person whose brain and spinal column have already begun to form."

"But I thought at this stage it was only lifeless tissue."

He pounded a fist into his palm. "Lifeless tissue doesn't have a beating heart. God says 'Before I formed you in the womb, I knew you.' Even now God knows this little child you're carrying. He can see the small depression that will be its ears." His voice rose with the intensity of his emotions. "He can identify the dark spots on the tiny head that will become the baby's eyes and nose."

She peered at him, tears trailing down her cheeks. "But what other answer do we have?"

Michael knew the truth then. He loved Tammy and wanted to marry her, giving their child a family. If she didn't believe in the Christian faith, he'd pray for her, everyday for the rest of his life if he had to. But he could never allow her to destroy their child. Sitting back down beside her, he gently held her hand in his. "Listen to me, Tammy. I want you to become my wife. We'll make a home for our baby."

She leaned away from him, as if his words were offensive. "But what about your family? They disapprove of me."

"That's only my brother, and he doesn't claim to honor God like the rest of us." Michael slipped to his knees in front of her. "My mom and dad will love you. Like I do." He cleared his voice. "This isn't going the way I had envisioned, but Tammy Crawford, will you please marry me? Say you'll take me as your husband."

Tammy stared at him for a long moment. She took a

shuddering breath and her eyes pooled with tears.

"What is it? What did I say?"

She lowered her head. Tears fell onto her jeans.

"I promise to offer you a proper proposal in a few weeks with a ring, but for now, tell me you'll say yes."

She took a deep breath and stood to walk to the kitchen bar. Snatching a tissue out of a box, she turned and faced him. "No, Michael. I could possibly get beyond your brother's hatred of me, but I've heard enough from Joella to know that your Christian family would be upset if they thought you were marrying someone who doesn't share your faith in God. I can't do that. It wouldn't be fair to you."

He neared her, holding her hands in his. "Tammy, in time …" He gulped. "But more than anything, I want to give our child a home."

"I understand, but right now, I want to be alone. Please go."

He leaned down to catch her teary gaze. "Tammy, do you love me?"

She slowly nodded, wiping away another tear. "More than you could know."

"Then let's get married."

Turning the knob, Tammy opened the door. "Love isn't always enough, Michael. Even I know that. If—if things were different." She shook her head. "But they're not."

"Please, Tammy. Listen to me. We can be happy together." He couldn't leave her like this.

She turned away from him. "I'm sorry."

There was no other choice but to go. The stride out the door seemed as if he stepped into a pot of boiling water. "We have to talk. Please don't do anything unless you talk to me first."

"Don't call me again." She held the tissue over her face. "It's best that way."

WHAT GOD KNEW

Chapter Seventeen

Tammy swallowed the nausea that threatened and pressed the *down* elevator button. She wasn't supposed to get sick in the afternoon. Time to go home, but her queasy stomach still hadn't given any relief.

With three days to put Michael's visit behind her, the memory of closing the apartment door after she'd asked him to leave, still tortured her. So final and she'd felt so alone. He'd texted her daily, but she'd made it plain. *Don't contact me again.*

The elevator doors slid open and she stepped inside. Another person occupied the space toward the back. Tammy averted her eyes, not feeling like conversing with anyone.

"Hey, friend. How's it going?" The cheery voice sounded all too happy.

Tammy lifted her gaze to the woman.

Glorilyn Neilson slipped her handbag's strap over her shoulder and beamed.

What was she so cheerful about? The door slid shut, and the elevator began the descent. "Hi, Glorilyn. How are you?" Maybe JD's sister would get off on the next floor. Tammy wasn't in the mood right now to chat with someone like her.

The young woman laid a hand over her heart. "I just finished my shift with The Cuddling Program in the neonatal clinic. It's such an asset to the Pediatrics Department."

Just the thought she didn't want to entertain right now—the NICU and especially one of the talented doctors. Had Michael been involved with initiating the program? From nowhere an image of him holding a tiny baby in his arms popped into her mind. Would he have made a good father? Thinking of him delivered an ache deep within her soul and caused her to face the truth. She was in love with him.

"I treasure each opportunity to hold one of those little babies in my arms. It's so important for infants to receive human touch in their first year of life," Glorilyn cooed.

The other woman's presence brought another wave of disquiet. Instinctively Tammy slipped her palm over her abdomen then gasped. Why had she done that? She wanted to hold and protect the baby—if it were really a living being. But if she followed her plan, he or she would never be held or rocked. Shaking her head, she dispelled the heartbreaking notion. If she were to get on with her life, she couldn't think like this. "Yes, I've read the studies as well. The hospital is lucky to have you and the others in the program."

Glorilyn laughed. "Did you know there are several guys who work in the program as well? Babies need masculine attention, too."

Tammy gripped the railing on the elevator wall. "I'm sure the neonatal department appreciates your time."

"It's not just these babies. I love all children." She laughed. "That's why I'm a kindergarten teacher. God cherishes little ones and says we have to be like one of them to enter His kingdom."

Next stop—ground floor. Tammy held her stomach and took a deep breath. "She couldn't get away from Glorilyn fast enough. She made Tammy more uncomfortable then sitting in church with Joella.

"Someday, I pray God will allow me to have one of my own."

Cold moisture dripped down Tammy's back. Why did Glorilyn have to go on and on about a baby? And why did her words make Tammy so miserable?

Finally the elevator came to a halt at the first floor and JD's sister marched out. "I enjoyed seeing you. Maybe you, me, and Joella can get together for lunch one of these days."

"Sounds good." Tammy's attempt to bring an enthusiastic lilt to her voice failed.

The young woman ambled out the front entrance toward the

parking lot.

Joella had mentioned several times that Glorilyn attended their church. Tammy assumed she held the same religious convictions as Joella and JD. Did her beliefs bring the optimism and even the peace on the young woman's face?

*****

Michael deposited his briefcase on the office desk and pulled out the folder packed with plans for the new hospital. He hadn't given full attention to the upcoming meeting with the potential board members, thinking of little more than the finality of the conversation with Tammy three days ago.

After several hours of walking the floor that night, he'd solidified the truth in his heart. He thought of her constantly and desired to protect her. Whether Tammy was pregnant or not, he needed to be with her always—praying she'd find the Savior one day.

He'd never have dreamed she would conceive that night, yet one mistake had resulted in life changing consequences. A small plastic testing device had bellowed the immutable truth. He shook his head at the irony. A doctor and a nurse. Two people in the medical field. Shouldn't they have known better?

A vision of a tiny baby glided into his brain. Their child. Who would he or she look like? Him or Tammy? He desired to hold and love this child someday, but Tammy had kicked him out of her apartment and said she saw no future for them. Did she intend to go on alone? How could he leave her single and pregnant? He was no better than the young studs his mother spoke about. The ones who used girls in the Augusta neighborhoods without thought for their welfare then took off. Too many children lived in fatherless homes.

Or had Tammy reverted to another plan? Anxiety shot through him. *Dear God, please don't allow her to take the life of our baby.*

More than ever, he regretted the night he slept with her. They should've given their relationship time to grow. He should've waited for her to find the Lord. Why hadn't he heeded the Holy Spirit's voice that night and remembered his Christian upbringing? He'd fallen flat on his face and didn't know if he could get up again.

Sure, he had God's forgiveness, but the scars of what he'd done wouldn't go away. If he could only convince Tammy that he loved her and wanted to make a home with her and their child, he'd be grateful. He took a cleansing breath. Wasn't God able to replace the ashes of his life with a crown of beauty? It would be easy to ignore the issue or fall into despair. But instead, Michael had the option to praise God.

God, You alone have the answers. I've run out of them. Please bring glory to Your name through my mistakes.

The wall clock indicated nine forty-five. Almost time to head over to the conference room Iris had booked for him. Still grateful for the ten people who'd agreed to come today, he snapped his briefcase shut with the folder containing copies he planned to pass out at the meeting. Hopefully the information would give potential board members a precise overview with the summary of the major points of the project. The short list of people who agreed to consider financially backing the hospital would be a start.

Michael nodded at Iris and walked out the door and down the hall to the conference room. As he neared, the sound of someone speaking over a microphone and the shuffle of papers met his ears. He frowned and approached the door. A sign said *Nine thirty to eleven thirty. American Hospital Association public service meeting—the future of healthcare in America.*

How could that be? Another meeting in his reserved room? He scrubbed a hand over his mouth.

"Good morning, Dr. Clark." The two men from TS Holdings, representatives of the venture capital firm he'd contacted, strolled toward him.

Michael shuffled his briefcase from one hand to the other. "I'm afraid there's been a mistake. I'd reserved this room but somehow another meeting seems to be taking place. If you'd like to walk with me back to my office, I'll speak to my secretary and clear up the matter." He tried to tamp down his growing irritation. Had Iris botched it again?

The two business men dressed in tailored suits shot a glance at each other then followed him back down the hall. The closer he got to the office, the more anger threatened to dominate his forthcoming words to Iris.

"Please wait here while I find out what's going on." Michael pointed to a couple of chairs outside the door.

Talking a deep breath, he walked in and tried not to glare or raise his voice as he spoke to her.

With a smile that wrinkled the corners of her eyes, she filed patient records in the metal cabinet and looked up at him.

He sucked in a deep breath. "Iris, did you book the conference room for me? I believe I asked you over a month ago?"

Her eyes widened. "Of course, Dr. Clark." She pulled out her desk calendar. "Oh, yes. Here's February." She looked down at the calendar and up to him. "Yes, it's for tomorrow at 10:00 a.m."

He gritted his teeth. "Iris, the meeting was supposed to be for today."

Her mouth went slack. "Oh? I thought I booked it on the right date." She pulled out a filing box for memos and thumbed through. "Let's see. February. Conference room." Her hand flew to her mouth. "Oh, I'm terribly sorry."

If Michael followed his gut reactions, he'd fire her today, but he had to calm down. He let out a long sigh and considered the alternatives. The conference room wasn't available. The small room off the main office would be cramped, but he had no choice except to hold the meeting there.

If this had been the first mistake she'd made, he'd overlook it in a heartbeat, but this had been the latest in a series of them.

Once again the kind, elderly woman had bungled an important assignment. He gazed at her face bearing the passages of time. No doubt Iris's intentions were good, but could he go on like this? Things needed to change, but how could he replace her? For his own sanity, he'd have to think of asking her to retire soon.

*****

At the end of the day, Michael took weary steps toward his Mercedes in the doctors' parking lot. Holding the meeting in the confined office space had made it hard to relax, but in the end, the news was good. Six men and four women had agreed to serve as board of directors for a period of one year with the promise to consider a longer term. The investors had indicated an interest.

The group's enthusiasm for a new children's hospital in El

Camino thrilled him. They'd all agreed that the growing El Camino community could support the specialty hospital.

He clicked the locks to his car and slid in, thoughts flying to Tammy. Somehow he had to convince her to talk to him. He pulled out on the street in front of the hospital calling Tammy's number on his Blue tooth. Her machine came on. Listening to her voice sent pangs of sadness to him. "Tammy, just talk to me. Give me a call."

A strong impression nudged him. *Go see Mom.* He swallowed with the involuntary gulp. Was that really a good idea? He didn't feel comfortable telling his mother about his mistakes. Yet maybe she could pray for him. He drove nearer his parents' neighborhood.

The street narrowed as he wound around past elegant estates. Each sat on expansive lots with ample acreage. When he parked in front of Mom and Dad's, he cringed as if waiting an injection with a long needle. Scraping his feet on the sidewalk, he trekked to the front door. This might be tougher than he thought.

Using his key to open the door, Michael walked into the large entryway. The aroma of pot roast led him to the kitchen.

Mom poked her head out before he stepped down the hall. "Oh, hello, Michael. This is a pleasant surprise."

It wouldn't seem too pleasant in only moments when he told her the truth. "Do you have a minute? Can we talk?"

Mom tossed her apron on the kitchen counter. "Sure. Dad's still out on the golf course, but if you'd like to talk to him, too, he'll be along after a while."

Talking to Dad? Best to speak to Mom first. "No, it's okay." Michael flopped down at the kitchen table, folding his wobbly legs underneath.

She pointed to the refrigerator. "Would you like a bottle of water?"

"No, no, thanks, Mom." The sooner they talked the better.

"The serious look on your face tells me you have something on your mind." Mom eased down at the table across from him. "I hope everything is okay."

Michael studied his hands on the table. *No, everything's not okay. My life has changed forever.* "I need to tell you something."

"Of course." She laid her hands over his. "You're welcome to say anything you'd like. Though you're a grown man, you'll always be my son."

Mom's quiet, Godly nature encouraged him. He patted her hand back. "I've got a problem. I need to bounce it off you."

Mom never took her gaze from his face. "I'm listening."

"I've been dating a nurse at the hospital."

"Yes, the white girl. The one Darnell mentioned at Christmas dinner."

He stared at the grain of the wood on the oak table.

"Your brother is obviously prejudiced against her. I certainly don't hold to his opinion. Please don't let his view worry you."

"I know, but … it's not that. I … we … made a mistake. Something I regret now. We slept together … once."

A melancholy smile appeared on her lips, reminding him of God's love for him though he had sinned. Mom understood yet disappointment was evident in her eyes. "Michael, God can forgive sexual sins, any kind of sin for that matter."

He shifted in his chair. "I know. But there's more. She's … she's expecting a baby."

Her composed demeanor wavered a moment as she took a few deep breaths. "I have to admit, I didn't expect you to say that." Mom lifted her fingers to touch her lips with well manicured nails. A wrinkle-free blouse graced her shoulders and arms as she crossed her legs at her ankles.

Shifting in his chair, he listened to only the sounds of the ticking clock from across the hall in the dining room and his own breathing. He nodded, waiting for her next words.

Her voice became a whisper. "Do you love her?"

He studied her soft brown eyes and lovely dark skin, curly white hair gracing her head. "Yes, with all my heart. But I'm afraid Tammy has booted me out of her life."

"Another important question." She lifted a finger. "Does she know the Lord?"

No surprise Mom would ask that question. He slowly moved his head from side to side. "She told me she didn't have faith in God like I do." Words stuck on the roof of his mouth. "More than Darnell's reaction to her, she's afraid that her lack of faith will put a wall between my family. Mom, I messed up."

Mom reached across the table and cupped his cheeks in both hands like she'd done in his childhood. "Look at me, Michael

James. I'll be honest. A mixed marriage could have its challenges, but there's something of greater importance. The problem isn't about race. Now it's about what is best for this child. It's about the hopelessness that comes when a girl of any color is left to raise her baby without a husband. It's about how two people can't survive in a tough situation without God."

Michael dropped his hands to his lap again as Mom folded hers. But his mother didn't know the rest of the story. Tammy could choose to take the child's life.

"This baby needs a father, and you can't do this without the Lord's intervention."

"Listen to me, Mom. I'm aware of that. I want to raise the child to know the Lord even if Tammy doesn't embrace our faith."

She stared at him without a word.

"But this gets much worse. Tammy is considering abortion." He blurted the words, each syllable knifing through him.

Tears filled Mom's eyes. "There's only One who can help. We need to pray in His name against this. God doesn't endorse abortion." Mom squeezed his hand. "Pray with me, Michael."

Strange how we seek God when we run out of answers, and He should be the One we turn to first. He nodded and closed his eyes.

Mom's quiet voice called out to the Lord. "Jesus, thank You that nothing is too hard for You. Despite the mistakes we make and the chaos of our lives, You are bigger. Michael is Your child, and we ask now in the name of Jesus, that You would spare this little life that Tammy carries. Touch Tammy's heart and allow her to seek Your salvation. Place someone in her path who she'll listen to. In the meantime, give my dear son wisdom about what he needs to do. In Jesus name."

Emotion threatened, but Michael wouldn't allow his mother to see vulnerability. He nodded and gazed into her eyes. "Thank you. Your prayer means more than I can say."

"Though we fail God, He's always faithful. Trust in Him. He'll work even this for your good."

Chapter Eighteen

The sign over the weatherworn brick building said *El Camino Women's Health Clinic*. Tammy paused in front of the double glass doors where she'd exited only moments ago. As if the place had cast a spell, she stood frozen to the sidewalk. As many times as she'd passed the location on her way to work, she'd never dreamed one day she'd avail herself of the clinic's services.

Now she'd taken the first step—verification of pregnancy and the appropriate blood tests. The results of the urine test had only required twenty minutes and confirmed the home test. As if Tammy needed a tooth filled or a checkup from the doctor, the woman spoke as if the abortion was an everyday occurrence. Maybe it was, but not for Tammy. "Make an appointment for the procedure in the next week or so. We'll help you dispose of this minor setback in your life," Mrs. Moriarty said.

Tammy pressed her cell phone's *on* button and glanced at the screen. Three missed calls, all from Michael. And those from today. His messages had begun two days ago.

The desperation in his voice almost convinced her she should at least talk to him. But she feared she'd listen to her heart instead of the facts. Maybe Michael would encourage her to marry him whether she believed as he did or not, saying it didn't matter. And what if he really wasn't in love with her but only acted out of a sense of duty? She pressed *off* again and slipped the phone in her purse.

The card the clinic manager had provided with her private

phone number lay at the bottom of Tammy's purse. "Call anytime," the woman had said. She reminded Tammy that her decision was the best option. Why allow a blob of tissue to disrupt her life? Her career came first.

When Tammy had confronted the woman about how the fetus had a heartbeat, Mrs. Moriarty had merely smiled and told Tammy that a heartbeat didn't make it a breathing, thinking person. It couldn't speak or survive outside the womb. It was called an embryo and a fetus for a reason, not a baby.

The manager seemed so confident in her thought process when she said medical science, philosophy, and religion all disagreed on the issue, and abortion was not murder. But did Tammy concur with the woman? Exhaling a stream of air didn't get rid of the anxiety racking her. Yet if she went through with the procedure, life would return to normal again in a few weeks. Wouldn't it?

She clicked the locks on her car where she'd parked behind the clinic and started the engine. Again—she reminded herself—the decision was a wise one. If the problem didn't go away, she'd be a mother by late September. She gripped the car's wheel until her fingers turned white.

Instead of driving home, she found herself on the way to Joella's neighborhood. Not to tell her about the baby—

Tammy's breath caught in her throat. A baby? When did the fetus actually become a person? Five months, seven? Opinions differed, yes, but surely not now at six weeks like Michael said. Though he was a doctor, his ideas originated from his prolife viewpoint.

Leaving the bustle of the downtown city streets, Tammy arrived at her sister's fashionable neighborhood. Why had she come? Though she would never embrace Joella's religion, Tammy had to admit, her sister seemed grounded, and Tammy needed that stability right now and her sister's love.

She brushed a tear away. Sure her hormones were raging now. If Mom were still alive, Tammy would've sought her out. But Mom was gone. Mopping her cheek with the back of her hand, Tammy wiped away the moisture that trailed down her face.

A smiling Joella opened the front door of their large, Spanish-style home. "Hey, little sis. Come on in." She gazed at Tammy, moving a little closer. "Are you okay?"

"Sure. Just tired." Hearing the words *little sis* brought with them a twinge of self pity, causing her to think of how her family had crumbled. "Thought I'd drop by on my way home from work to see how everything's going?" Since Tammy didn't usually visit, would Joella wonder why she'd come?

"Great. JD's working on a project at church and took the baby, so we've got the place all to ourselves." She waved her hand toward the living room then squeezed Tammy's arm. "How about something to drink? Or some of the chicken noodle soup I made JD for supper?"

Though Tammy hadn't expected her sister to feed her, the offer sounded wonderful. "My stomach is growling a little. I skipped lunch today."

Joella looked her up and down. "What am I going to do with you? You're bone thin now. You need to eat to stay healthy."

Though most pregnant women said they were eating for two, that wouldn't be true much longer for Tammy. She followed Joella to the kitchen, her hungry stomach urging her on.

Joella pointed to the contemporary Danish-style kitchen table with matching chairs. "Sit down. The soup's ready. How about a piece of homemade sourdough bread with butter?"

Just the suggestion of the meal made Tammy's mouth water. She laughed. "If I ate like this every night, maybe I'd gain a little weight. I have to admit, my scrubs are hanging on me now."

Joella dipped a ladle into the large pot and poured a helping of soup in a ceramic bowl. "What do you make for yourself when you get off work?"

"Honestly, since it's just me, not much. A lot of times I eat a sandwich or a frozen meal. No point in cooking for only one." The night she'd made dinner for Michael remained in her memory—the night that had changed her life.

Joella winked and set the steaming hot bowl in front of her and then scooped a bowl for herself. "Well, what about that handsome doctor? If he's the one, maybe you'll be cooking for two someday."

Tammy sucked in a breath and held it. Joella had no idea the thorny subject she'd broached. Though Tammy had always believed herself an independent career woman, what would it be like to share her life with Michael? What would it hurt to allow the daydream for a moment?

"Tammy, you're a million miles away?"

"I'm sorry." Tammy shook her head and focused on Joella. "No, I'm not seeing Michael anymore. Things weren't progressing very well." A boldface lie. Things had progressed way too far, way too fast, and she carried the consequences.

"Oh, I take it he's not the one." Joella set a couple of thick slices of hot bread and a butter dish on the table.

"I don't know."

Joella's world included a man she adored and a happy marriage. Even if Michael truly loved Tammy, did they belong together? Could they survive the challenges of his disapproving family and his religion? "Hey, sis. When did you first realize you'd fallen in love with JD, and how did you know he was it?"

A dreamy expression fell over Joella's face. "I think the first time I knew was when I stopped to think how many times JD put me first and came to my rescue. After we started dating, he'd patiently listen to me when I poured out all my work problems. Once when a client attacked me, he got furious and wanted to confront the guy. He was so protective. I could tell—he really loved me."

Michael said he loved her, though she might be foolish to believe it.

But thoughts of him persisted anyway. They hadn't dated a long time like Joella and JD did before they married, but Tammy could remember when Michael stood up for her. Like the night with Darnell at Giorgio's. And he'd expressed genuine interested in her plans to study for a NP degree. She couldn't deny the way he'd looked at her a few times, as if she were the only woman in the world.

"From the start, I could never fathom myself married to anyone else." Joella dabbed her chin with a napkin. "I wanted to spend my life with him and have his children. When he finally broke free of the cult in which he'd grown up and trusted the Lord in his life, the door opened wide for us to marry. Now, God is at the center of our life together."

But what about her and Michael? She hadn't made a commitment to Jesus like he had. Joella's words echoed the same sentiments Tammy held about the handsome doctor. She wanted to spend her life with him as well. Tears clogged her throat. Yet marriage to Michael didn't seem probable.

Joella's face paled, and she clasped a hand over her mouth. "Excuse me." She darted out of the room. Maybe the soup hadn't agreed with her.

About ten minutes later, Tammy's sister returned to the kitchen. "Sorry, sis." She eased back down at the table dabbing her nose with a tissue. "Listen, only JD knows so far, but we have some awesome news. There's a new Neilson on the way. I'm six weeks pregnant."

Six weeks? Tammy gulped down the gasp that tried to escape from her throat. Joella couldn't know she was also pregnant. "Oh, that's... er, wonderful."

"When I first found out I was expecting Jacob, I'd marveled at God's great creation, the tiny baby within me." Joella placed her hand on her abdomen. "Now He's seen fit to give us another."

Tammy's mouth went dry. From under the table, she slid a hand over her own stomach. The clinic manager called it a blog of tissue. Joella referred to it as a tiny new life. Who should she believe? A wave of grief and loss inundated her. *Mom, why did you have to leave us? I need you right now.*

*****

Tammy dragged herself out of her apartment and to her car. After throwing up twice this morning, she'd expended all her energy, and the day had only begun.

On automatic pilot, she drove toward town and the hospital. She'd never felt so unsure before. She'd always prided herself in taking charge of life. Is this why some people became Christians? Was it easier to trust God with things?

But no, dependency didn't define her. The solution seemed plain now. She needed to go through with the procedure at the Women's Health Center.

A city bus crept along in front of her, and she drummed her fingers on the steering wheel as traffic slowed to a turtle's pace. Sure Joella called it a baby, a tiny life, but that originated with her religious beliefs. Though her sister's sentiments had begun to make sense two days ago, Tammy no longer saw the logic. The thing inside wasn't a baby and marriage wasn't the answer.

Thy will be done on earth as it is in Heaven. Tammy shook her head. A snippet from the Lord's Prayer she'd learned in Sunday school tiptoed into her thoughts. Odd.

As her phone rang, she glanced at the caller ID. Michael. Again. Shoving her phone in her purse, she switched on a jazz CD. She didn't want to talk to him or to anyone.

*****

That night, Tammy booted up her computer at the kitchen table and clicked on e-mails. After reading the one at the top of the list, she let out a yelp. The scholarship. The American Association of Nurse Practitioners would be happy to grant her financial aid for the duration of her online studies that included practical training at El Camino General.

The acceptance notice said Tammy's high GPA in nursing school and her years of experience were the determining factor in the group's decision. The news confirmed everything she believed about achieving one's goals—people could only depend on themselves to get what they wanted. She'd worked hard all those years, and now she would reap the fruit of her labor.

A scholarship. Good news, right? Tammy leaned back in the chair and shook her head as reality slapped her in the face. How could she concentrate on school with a baby? Since her grant only covered the cost of classes, she'd have to continue working at the hospital to support herself and the child, if she went through with things.

Face it. She couldn't physically perform the duties of a geriatrics RN if she was nine months along.

She snapped her laptop closed and rose from her chair, pacing the room. The decision to end the pregnancy solidified in her mind once again. She couldn't abandon her plans and her career now.

When the phone rang, Michael's name appeared on her screen. Not daring to talk to him, she clicked her cell phone off. One day he'd get tired of calling.

Chapter Nineteen

Michael flew into the hospital parking lot which was lit only by pole lamps. He parked, charged out of the car, and slammed the driver's door behind him. For the staff to notify him to return immediately to the neonatal unit meant only one thing—a baby in distress.

Unable to focus on little else, the message from Jerry Taylor hadn't sounded good. The Michelfelder's twenty-five week preemie showed signs of respiratory complications. The child might lose his battle.

Rushing from the lot, he headed into the building. When he stepped onto the elevator, he took a deep breath. God's presence filled him now more than ever before. *Lord, please grant me wisdom in providing the best care I can.*

The elevator door opened to the seventh floor. He glanced at his watch and hurried toward the NICU. A solemn faced Jerry met him before he reached baby Michelfelder's crib.

She shook her head. "When the baby first went into respiratory distress, we called the parents. They're on their way. We followed all the normal NICU procedures. I'm sorry. The baby expired five minutes ago. Our efforts to revive him failed. I need you to confirm the death."

Michael's heart sank. The news he dreaded hearing. "All right, Jerry. Thanks." As long as he practiced medicine, he'd never get used to a child's death. Retaining an air of professionalism and separating himself emotionally from the patient, proved to be more difficult every regretful time.

After examining the child's lifeless body and filling out the paper work, Michael stepped over to the nurse's station and glanced at his watch again. He handed the paper work to Jerry. "The parents should be here in a minute. I'll meet with them."

She nodded. "Thank you, Doctor."

Down the hall, the elevator doors opened, and the couple rushed toward him.

God, give me the strength. Before Michael could open his mouth, the wide-eyed parents neared, Mrs. Michelfelder clutching her husband's arm.

Michael steeled himself. "I'm so sorry. We lost him a few minutes ago." Fighting the temptation to give into the sorrow building in his gut, Michael straightened to his full height.

Mrs. Michelfelder stared in stunned silence then covered her face. She buried her head in her husband's chest and sobbed.

The dark-haired man gulped. "We got here as fast as we could after we were called."

"Yes, sir. I understand. No one had anticipated this."

"What happened to our son?"

"As a micro preemie, your son faced a unique set of challenges. He suffered from RDS or Reparatory Distress Syndrome. Difficulty breathing due to underdeveloped lungs. This is a common cause of infant death. The Nurse Practitioner and her staff did all they could."

Mr. Michelfelder's shoulders shook as he held his wife with one arm and placed a fist over his eyes with the other.

How would Michael have reacted if the child was his? He gripped the man's arm. The death of any infant was undoubtedly one of life's most difficult tragedies.

Mrs. Michelfelder turned from her husband. "Can ... can we see him?"

"Of course," Michael said.

Jerry walked up to them. "If it helps, you can find closure by spending time with the infant, perhaps rocking him and taking a picture."

The grieving wife glanced up at her husband. "Robbie, I need that."

As if a knife stabbed him, Michael tightened his jaw then

nodded. "Come this way."

Planted to the floor, Mr. Michelfelder didn't take a step and glared at Michael. "Wait. Did you say the nurse practitioner was with him when he passed? You weren't there?" Mr. Michelfelder's voice rose to a bellow.

"No. I came as soon as I was notified."

"If my baby was that close to death, you should've been there." Now the man yelled. "I see no excuse."

This response was all too common, especially with grieving fathers. Anger had replaced grief. "The child had been stable when I left this afternoon, sir. I'm terribly sorry, but I doubt my presence would've changed things. Our nursing staff is extremely competent." How else could he comfort them?

The Christian faith taught that when a child dies, he or she goes immediately to be in God's presence. He generally didn't speak of doctrine with a parent, but if he could offer any scrap of hope, he would. "I can't imagine the extent of your grief, but I want you to know, your little boy is safe with God now. Please take comfort in that."

"You think you can placate us with your ridiculous platitudes?" Mr. Michelfelder scowled as he balled his fists. "Trying to cover your rear, the neglect of your duties with fairy tales." He grabbed Michael's lab jacket and shook him, the irate father's face no more than three inches away. "Your incompetence is appalling." Tears ran down his cheeks.

Michael stepped back from the aggressive, grieving man. "Try to calm yourself, Mr. Michelfelder. If you'd like to go ahead to visit with your baby, that might be best." Though there was little more Michael could say, he'd continue to pray for them. "I'll be here if you need me."

*****

For three days, Michael hadn't been able to put aside the image of the inconsolable couple when they'd arrived at the NIC unit. He sank back into the office chair and covered his eyes, praying once again for the parents.

Then the persistent fear jabbed him again. His child, though unborn, might be in danger as well.

What had Tammy decided? She'd said abortion was an option. Had she chosen to end the child's life?

He was desperate to talk to her. For the tenth time, he pulled out his cell and punched in the speed-dial number. If she didn't answer this time, he'd go to her apartment when he left the hospital.

As usual, the machine picked up. "Tammy, it's me again. We need to talk. I love you. Call me."

He glanced at his watch. In a half hour, he'd head to her house and camp out at her door if necessary.

*****

In the hall, Michael pounded on Tammy's door after ringing the bell. No answer.

From the apartment beside hers, a muscular man sporting a heavy five o'clock shadow and a scowl stepped out into the hall and growled. "Is there something I can help you with?"

Michael winced. Now he was disturbing the neighbors.

From the way the guy looked him up and down then focused on Michael's face, he wondered what part of his appearance he questioned. "No, thank you. I'm looking for Tammy Crawford."

"What do you want Tammy for?" He growled again.

"Oh, I just need to talk to her, and I can't get her on the phone. I'll leave a note." Sitting in the hall didn't seem like a good idea now. The way the bodybuilder of a guy glared, it made Michael feel like a kid again when the teacher assumed he didn't know how to spell.

"Humph." The burly dude stomped back inside his home.

Michael scrubbed a hand over his mouth and pulled a scrap of paper from his pocket. He scribbled. "Tammy, I need to talk to you. It's imperative. Michael." He slid it under her door and turned to walk down the hall, hands shoved in his pockets. *Lord, I'm at a loss here.*

Chapter Twenty

Michael finished his rounds and turned to the nurses' station where Charlotte feverishly tapped away on the computer keys. After leaving Tammy's apartment two days ago, it became apparent. There was no use in trying to phone or leave a note. She wasn't about to answer.

Since the preemies were all stable, he'd leave the floor for a moment. If he made a quick trip to geriatrics, hopefully he could see Tammy. He didn't want to embarrass her, but if this was the only way to talk to her, he had to do it.

As he drew nearer, Charlotte's phone rang, and she picked up. "Yes, ma'am. A total of four visitors for each baby as long as at least one parent is present." She nodded. "You're welcome." She hung up and peered at him. "Is everything okay on the floor, Dr. Clark? You look worried."

Did he wear his feelings on his face like a banner? He forced a smile. "No, everything's fine. Our patients' vital signs are good. Be back in fifteen minutes. Page me if needed." He wished he felt as confident as he sounded.

"Of course, Doctor." She nodded then turned to the ringing phone again.

After he stepped into the elevator, he swallowed hard and pressed the *down* button. He didn't want to interfere with Tammy's duties in any way, but he'd offer a quick invitation to join him for lunch at the cafeteria as they'd done a month ago.

Getting out on the fourth floor, he firmed his jaw and strode toward a group of nurses at the counter. He expected to see Tammy sitting there, but instead a blonde in pink scrubs whose nametag said *Beth Logan, RN*, glanced up. "Yes, Doctor. May I help you?"

He rubbed his neck and pushed a smile in place. "I need to speak with Tammy Crawford, please. Is she with a patient at the moment?" If he had to wait a bit, he would.

She shook her head. "No, she called in sick today."

"Sick?" Would nausea due to pregnancy keep her from work or was it something else, an appointment at the women's clinic? " Dread filled him. "All right. Thanks." If it were possible, he'd leave the hospital right then and make a trip to her apartment. But he couldn't abandon his shift. And who knew if she'd answer the door.

The larger doctors' lounge where he'd first met Tammy was down the hall from the geriatrics unit. His heavy steps clunked on the tiled floor as he made his way to there.

After pouring himself a cup of coffee, he paced the room with its comfortable couches and coffee bar. Today it didn't provide an oasis to unwind, though. He almost spilled the hot drink on his lab jacket. What could he do now? He needed counsel. Someone who knew Tammy's family. Not from his family or Jeff Valentine but a Christian minister.

Since the space was deserted, he pulled out his cell and located the list of contacts. He scrolled down to the *R's* and punched Dave Reyes' work number then waited.

*****

Michael walked out of his office and returned to the NICU, grateful Dave had been able to schedule him for later this afternoon. The thought of sharing his burden with another Christian man offered his heavy heart hope.

The newest preemie born at twenty-nine weeks lay in the incubator nearest his office. He stepped to the baby girl's crib and glanced down at her. Positioning the tips of his stethoscope in his ears, he lightly glided it along her tiny body between her neck and waist.

She raised a small fist into the air.

With a gloved hand, he extended one finger, and she gripped

it. The minute features of her face, a perfectly formed nose, blonde eye lashes, ears the size of small shirt buttons fascinated him. Though scientific data of human reproduction explained the process, ultimately God fashioned new life. He made her beating heart and placed it inside her body, causing it to beat thirty-one million times in one year. Her circulatory and digestive systems were nothing more than miraculous. Humans were merely incubators for God's incredible plan of creating people.

An idea formed in his mind. Maybe he could describe to Tammy his vision of what their child would look like—to help her understand that their baby was indeed a person. He'd do it at the first available opportunity if he could find a way to see her.

More than ever, Michael was grateful for a connection with his Lord. Though life challenged him now, the underlying peace God placed in his soul sustained him.

Once again, he drew his attention to the fragile, helpless girl in front of him. *Dear God. I pray You will nurture this child that she may grow strong. In Jesus name.*

After completing his exam and marking her chart, he returned to his office. His growling stomach gave a noisy reminder that it was almost time for lunch. He'd hoped to eat with Tammy today, but now he'd go alone to the cafeteria.

He checked his in-house e-mails and printed off one from a potential board member.

His cell phone rang, and he pulled it out of his pocket. The caller ID said Darnell. "Hey, Bro. What's up?"

"Hi, Michael. I really need to talk to you. Are you free for lunch?"

He hesitated. The only time his brother wanted to speak with him lately was to present his radicalized thinking, but Michael needed to open up the lines of communication. Someday Darnell might come to his senses. "Yeah, I was just thinking about heading down to the cafeteria."

"I'm seeing a client not too far from the hospital. How about if I meet you in ten minutes?"

"Sure. See you there."

*****

Michael set his tray loaded with a tuna sandwich, apple slices, and a large salad, on a table near the entrance as Darnell eased down opposite him.

His brother furrowed his brow and lifted his gaze to Michael's face. "Thanks for having lunch with me today."

"Sure. You look concerned about something. Are you okay? Not getting sick or anything?"

"No. Not at all." Darnell took a sip of iced tea. "What kind of a brother would I be if I sat quietly aside and let you make the biggest mistake of your life?"

"Darnell, can't we have one meal where we don't discuss racial bias. I'd just like to enjoy your company."

"I realize you've got the hots for that white woman. You're interested in more than just discussing the latest *American Journal of Medicine*. But try to put your life in perspective. In the long run, it would never work. You know that. Please don't brush me off this time."

Obviously Darnell perceived Michael's relationship with Tammy as sensual, which was far from the truth now. More and more he understood his deepening feelings. His brother had no idea that Michael could actually be in love with the Caucasian nurse. "Look, man, you just don't get it." Michael placed a napkin in his lap. "Love is about two people wanting to spend the rest of their lives together. It's not about the color of skin, but about the admiration they have for each other."

Darnell pounded his fist on the table, and their plates rattled. "You've got it all wrong. You'll regret it if you marry that woman." He shook his finger in Michael's face. "Look, is there anything at all I can say to dissuade you from pursuing her?"

The forceful words delivered a jab of anger, and Michael balled his fists. His brother had no business telling him what to do. Especially since his advice was opposite of everything Michael's heart proclaimed. "No, nothing."

Darnell rose to his feet. "All right. I'm done talking. I can't sit around and watch you do this to yourself." Without turning around, his brother stomped through the crowded cafeteria toward the exit without eating one bite of his food.

Michael's gaze followed Darnell's angry form until he was out of sight. Michael had sensed a threat in his siblings parting words.

He prayed his brother knew where to draw the line on his actions.

*****

Michael pulled up in front of the sprawling church where Dave Reyes served as pastor. A sign in front directed him to a side door and Dave's office down a long hall. With every step, part of Michael's burden seemed to lift.

The office to the right was empty and the lights off.

"Hi, Michael." Dave's voice called as he neared from the other end of the corridor. Catching up, the pastor extended his hand, a wide grin on his face.

"I hope I didn't keep you after office hours." Michael pointed to the glass windows. "I see the main office is closed."

"No, I had work I needed to catch up on. Betty Ann's not expecting me for dinner for at least another hour." He circled around and walked the way he'd come. "Come on back."

"How's little Abby?" Michael followed Dave down the hall.

Dave extended a hand when they entered the elegant space with a tall bookcase on one wall and framed diplomas on the other. "She's growing as fast as the dahlias in our garden last summer, and she's sleeping through the night. For a while, Betty Ann and I thought we'd never get a full night's sleep ever again."

"I suppose that's the joy of having a new born." Michael settled into the elegant upholstered chair across from Dave and folded his hands. He needed to talk to Dave about Tammy. How should he best frame the words? He studied his fingers in his lap.

"I'm sure you're not making a house call." Dave laughed. "How can I help you, Doctor? From the look on your face, I'd say you have something on your mind."

Michael lifted his gaze to Dave's kind face, his dark brown eyes sparkling. The guy radiated inner peace. "You're right. I'm here to speak to you as a pastor."

"You got it, buddy." Dave propped his leg over his knee and leaned back in the chair. "What can I do for you?"

"First, I need to tell you—I was raised a Christian and love the Lord but stumble in my walk sometimes." He dropped his gaze to the floor and shook his head. This was harder than he thought. Lifting his chin again, Michael peered at the other man.

Dave's face lit from his eyes to his mouth. "Let me assure you. We all do. None of us will be perfect until we see Him face to face. But I admire you. It's humbling to admit our failures. Especially as men. We tend to believe we have to maintain control and solve all life's problems."

"True." Talking to Dave had seemed daunting, but now part of the apprehension left. "But there's something I need to bounce off you."

"I'm listening, friend."

"I fell in love with someone this last winter."

"That doesn't sound like a bad thing." Dave grinned.

"Yeah, but I ignored an important aspect of the relationship. The spiritual side of our lives. After several dates and a growing attraction to her, I finally brought up the subject of her beliefs. She was honest and told me she wasn't walking with the Lord." Michael couldn't say more, especially that he'd already gotten Tammy pregnant.

Though he didn't mind confessing his mistake to the pastor, he wouldn't betray her by revealing the information behind her back, even if Dave kept it confidential.

"I can understand what happened, but let me tell you what the Word says. We're not to be unequally yoked with unbelievers. That applies to intimate relationships with others, in particular a husband or wife."

"So you're saying it would be wrong to marry this woman."

"Let me tell you a story. When I first met Betty Ann, she had just come out of a vicious non-Christian cult that believed the only way to achieve status in Heaven was to do good works in this lifetime. Though she no longer claimed allegiance to the group, she was confused about what she believed. And the hard part for me was I fell in love with her."

"What happened?"

"It was the most difficult thing I've ever done, but I had to give Betty Ann over to God. I wanted to be obedient to Him first."

Michael squirmed in the chair hoping Dave didn't notice. *Yeah, but Betty Ann wasn't pregnant, and you had time to wait on the Lord.*

"But when Betty Ann experienced a life-threatening event, she called on God and He answered her. Shortly after, she realized her need for salvation and prayed with me to give her life to Jesus. I can't help but believe my prayers and those of others had something to do with it. God worked it out in His own way and in His own timing."

Dave's story had a happy ending, but Michael's situation had been complicated by sex before marriage. "Another thing, Dave. She's white and some members of my family are very much against a mixed racial marriage."

"I'll admit, brother. That's a tough place to be. But I've got good news. All things are possible with our Lord. We serve a big God. He says to cast all our cares on Him because He cares for us. I'm not trying to sound like a preacher here, and I personally know how hard it is to love someone yet not be sure you'll ever have a future together."

"I'm sure I don't have to ask twice, but please keep everything I've told you in confidence." Michael peered at Dave.

"You can be assured what we say goes no further."

Michael clenched his jaw. "You know her." He wanted nothing more than to reveal the entire story, but again, he'd made up his mind to protect Tammy.

"You're not obligated to identify her."

"I know. But I want you to be aware so you can pray for her. She's Joella Neilson's sister. She was at the baby dedication and your home."

"Yes, Joella and I have been friends since college. I've known Joella's sister, Tammy, since she was in high school." He chuckled. "Joella always spoke about her as independent and self-willed. I understand now she's a skilled geriatrics nurse at the hospital. Her determination has brought her the tools she needed to achieve."

"To say the least. Please pray for me."

"Would you like to pray right now?"

Michael nodded and bowed his head.

After Dave finished his prayer, Michael stood. "Thanks for seeing me."

"Come back soon and let me know how things are going. In the meantime, I'll keep you in my prayers daily."

Michael held out his hand for a handshake. "Thanks, Dave." With a heavy gait, he trudged out of the office and returned to his car. When he clicked the locks on the Mercedes, he had the compelling urge to kick himself. Now he wished he'd told Dave the whole story, despite revealing his and Tammy's secret. Somehow it seemed best. Perhaps Dave would agree with Mom when he knew all the facts. Marry Tammy and provide his child a home with both a mother and father. But how could he if she wouldn't say yes?

Starting the motor, he tapped a closed fist on the dashboard, resisting the urge to go back to New Life Fellowship. Now he was convinced. He needed to tell Dave the truth.

He took a deep breath. Not today, but in a couple of weeks he'd reveal the rest of the story.

WHAT GOD KNEW

Chapter Twenty-One

Michael paced his office once again, his cell phone plastered to his ear. *Ring, ring.* Why did he expect Tammy would answer this time when she'd avoided him for days? "Hello, this is Tammy. Leave me a message."

Why bother to say anything? Michael clicked the *off* button. Attempting to count the number of messages he'd left, he ran out of fingers. *Okay, tonight I'll try her apartment again, even if the neighbor scowls at him. She's bound to answer the door sometime. If I have to, I'll wait out in my car all night.*

The rapping on his office door jerked him back from his frustrations and doubts. "Yes, come in, please."

Dr. Valentine poked his head in. "Got a minute, Michael?" He peered at him, his brow furrowed.

A concern about one of the patients, undoubtedly. "Sure, Jeff. Come in." He pointed to the chair near his desk. "Have a seat."

He edged down into the leather office chair. "Thanks. I need to consult with you a moment about a new arrival to the unit earlier today. I'm getting ready to go off shift."

Michael rolled his desk chair around and sat adjacent to him. "Another new admission?"

"Yeah. Around 6:00 this morning. The full-term baby came up from the birthing center. The gynecologist who delivered the seven-pound boy suspects possible hyperbilirubinemia—perhaps conjugated Type III and requested the child to be placed in the NICU unit for testing and observation." Jeff rested his ankle over his knee. "I examined the baby earlier. I believe it could be Dublin-Johnson Type II in which case we don't need to worry."

"All right, Jeff. Thanks for the update. I'll keep an eye on his serum bilirubin levels and the coproporphyrin I in his urine. Let's pray its only Type II."

Jeff stood. "Okay, buddy." He stretched his shoulders and smothered a yawn. "I'm going home to get some sleep. It's been a long night." Jeff meandered toward the door then turned around again, a grin on his face. "How are things progressing with the nurse? That day in the cafeteria, you looked like you were ready to take her home to meet the family."

A lump formed in Michael's throat. No way he could tell Jeff about how he'd gotten Tammy pregnant, and she was considering abortion. "There are a few complications right now." Michael scratched the back of his neck.

"Okay, well, if it's meant to be, I'm sure things will work out." He slapped Michael on the back and walked out of the office.

Meant to be? Jeff's words echoed in his mind. Would he and Tammy marry and raise their child together? He couldn't ignore his own doubts that inundated him.

Michael sat back down in his office chair and bowed his head. On the floor, at-risk babies received expert medical treatment. The staff took every precaution to improve their lives. And yet some people chose to destroy these helpless little babies before birth, never offering them a chance to thrive. "Dear Lord," he whispered. "Please give me wisdom as I examine our new patient. Please take care of the other child, too—the one Tammy carries. Her baby—and mine."

*****

In the afternoon, Michael finished his examination of the patient Jeff spoke about. Satisfied the baby could be diagnosed with the harmless Type II Hyperbilirubinemia, he released a breath. The lab results would solidify his findings. He marked the child's chart and headed toward the nurses' desk.

Long ago, he'd mastered the art of centering his thoughts solely on his patients, but today he had to forcibly shoo away the nagging remembrance of Jeff's visit and his question about

Tammy, invoking his fears and doubts about their relationship.

A smiling Charlotte Sperry hung up the phone and grinned at him.

"Charlotte, when the lab reports come back on the new admission, the full term baby, please let me know as soon as possible."

"Of course. I'll leave a note for the night nurse as well."

He replaced his pen in his lab coat pocket. "Thanks."

She smiled at him. "Do you ever check out the hospital review sites online? I saw a bunch of glowing appraisals of the NICU. Some of them were about you. I think you might be nominated for sainthood pretty soon."

"I don't think I've seen them." Michael laughed. "But sainthood? Not so sure about that." He shook his head and turned back to his office, not allowing Charlotte to see his fading smile.

Charlotte had intended to give him a compliment, but instead, shame washed over him. Sure Michael had been instrumental in saving premature babies, but he had no control over saving his own child.

Chapter Twenty-Two

Tammy pulled into her parking space at the apartment and turned off her headlights. Working late tonight had worn her out. She leaned back on the seat and closed her eyes a moment, remembering Michael's note he'd slipped under her door. Once again, she vowed it would be best not to talk to him. Though her decision might be unfair, she feared facing him. He'd try to convince her everything would work out, and she knew differently.

She opened her eyes and lifted the door handle. Who said life was fair anyway? Was it fair that Mom died or that Tammy wound up pregnant? Pushing the door open with more force than necessary, she exited the car and marched toward the front of the building.

From the corner of her eye, she spied a shadowy figure approaching. Probably one of the tenets returning home late as well. She glanced toward the person, possibly an African-American man, as he neared with a quickened pace. Her heart pounded with fear. Was he going to attack her? Should she make a run for it?

The shape suddenly morphed into someone who looked familiar. Michael. She froze. But she wasn't ready to see him.

Yet her heart told her she needed him. To hold her, to be there for her.

She stopped on the sidewalk about thirty feet from the entrance and watched as Michael walked nearer. When he came within ten feet, her breath caught in her throat. Though no moonlight shone tonight, she made out the man's features. The person approaching her was not Michael Clark.

"Tammy? Do you have a minute?"

Her hand flew to her chest. Did he mean her harm, and how did he know her name? Sheer curiosity overcame her, and she waited until he stood facing her. "Yes, do I know you?"

"We met once. At Giorgio's. Regretfully, I wasn't myself that night. I need to apologize for my behavior."

"Darnell?" The resemblance in his features told her he and Michael were brothers.

"Yes." He stuck out his hand. "I'm Darnell Clark. I just need a minute."

Michael didn't introduce them the night at Giorgio's, he but must've mentioned her name to the family later. "How did you know where I live?" Surely, Michael hadn't provided her address.

He touched his hands together in a prayer position. "Please don't think I'm a stalker or something, but I intended to talk to you at the hospital, but before I had the chance, you were in your car driving out of the parking lot. I followed you from there. It was the only way. It's important I talk to you."

No way would Tammy invite him into her home. For a moment, unease sent blaring reminders that this man didn't like her, despite his friendly manner. He wouldn't dare attack her, would he? "Okay." She shifted from one foot to the other.

His piercing dark eyes narrowed to slits as he peered at her. "I need to warn you."

Tammy frowned. What was this guy up to? "I'm afraid I don't know what you're talking about."

Dropping his chin, he stared at his feet and scraped the heel of his boot on the sidewalk. "This is hard for me to say, but I'm only looking out for your best interest." He took a deep breath.

Tammy stifled the chuckle that threatened to emerge. Why would this man care about her best interests?

"I'm aware that you and Michael have been dating. You need to understand something about our family."

"Your family?"

"Yes. Our father carries a deep-seated prejudice. He's against his children getting involved in a relationship with... " He coughed. "I suppose I better lay this out and not mince words. Dad is opposed to his children and grandchildren marrying out of their race. In fact, I've heard him say that if one of us did marry a white, he'd turn his back on them, kicking them out of the family, as if he'd never been born."

But Darnell had expressed his negative sentiments the night at Giorgio's. Wasn't he actually trying to blame his father for his own opinions or did racial prejudice extend to Mr. Clark as well? Tammy tipped her head to one side, glaring at him. "What about you? I heard what you said the night I met you."

He thrust his hands in his pockets. "I was drunk, but even so, I agree with my father's opinions. Honestly, there are difficulties when whites and blacks marry. But my beliefs aren't important. It's Dad's that are. I'm sure you wouldn't want to stand in the way of our mother never getting to see her son again. And that's what would happen if you and Michael continue this relationship."

And she'd never get to see her grandchild that Tammy carried, either. A knot twisted her stomach escalating the threatening nausea. "I see your point, Darnell. I wouldn't want to be responsible for breaking up a family."

"I'm glad you understand."

Could Michael's brother be exaggerating or outright lying about his father's way of thinking? She closed her eyes and pressed a hand to her forehead. She couldn't be sure, but the odds were Mr. Clark didn't approve of her either.

Michael's father. One more roadblock to a relationship with Dr. Clark—not counting her own doubts. She batted at the tear that escaped as Darnell strolled back to his vehicle on the other side of the street.

*****

Tammy kicked off her shoes and headed toward the kitchen for a bottle of water. Collapsing on the couch, she turned on the TV. Anything to take her mind off the disturbing encounter with Darnell.

She closed her eyes as drowsiness and fatigue washed over her.

Knock, knock. Tammy started up from the sofa and glanced at her watch. A full hour had escaped since she'd spoken with

Michael's brother.

The commentator on the weather channel warned of a snowstorm about to hit the northeast. She switched off the TV and listened.

Ring, ring. The doorbell. Maybe Darnell came back again to convince her to stay away from his brother. She dragged her tired body toward the door and looked through the peep hole. Yep, Darnell again. But how did he know which apartment was hers? She peeked again, and this time saw Michael's handsome face filled with worry.

Tempted not to answer, she rested her head on the front door. Then Darnell's threats challenged her. She'd find out the truth about Michael's family. Tammy unlatched the lock, inching the door open.

Michael, wringing his hands, stared at her, desperation evident on his face. "Oh, thank God. May I come in?"

Pushing the door open a little farther, she stepped back. "Yes. I need to talk to you, too."

Michael rushed into the living room looking from side to side. He circled around and gaped at her. "For days now— " His chest heaved. "Tammy, why wouldn't you answer my calls and notes?"

Voices from out in the hall distracted her. Residents returning home, no doubt, from a day at work.

She turned back to Michael, questioning what she'd say. "It's hard to explain." *Stand strong, Tammy.* Don't look at his pleading deep-brown eyes.

Darnell's hardened expression contrasted to the glowing concern on Michael's face.

"I dropped by the geriatrics floor the other day. They said you were sick. Are you okay?"

She nodded. "Yeah, I'm fine." Other than tired and nauseous. She pointed to the couch. "Sit down."

Michael edged onto the sofa, and Tammy sat across from him in the occasional chair. Keeping her distance seemed like a good idea.

He rested his hand on the couch. "How are you feeling now?"

"I'll be okay soon. I probably won't be pregnant much longer." The second the words shot from her mouth, she wanted to call them back. Now she'd broken her promise to herself not to reveal the plans to him.

He rushed up from the couch and knelt down in front of her, smoothing his hand over hers. "I know you don't believe me, but I love you, and I love our unborn child. Please don't go through with this."

For a moment she wanted to give into the look of anguish on his face and his tender touch.

"Listen to me." Michael gripped both her hands in his. "The other day I pictured what our baby would look like. He or she would probably have my curly dark hair and perhaps your green eyes. Tammy, he would be the most beautiful baby in the world with a little round face and tan cheeks. I want to marry you and raise this child in a home with a father and mother." His voice broke with the emotion.

What if they married and ten years from now he realized he didn't love her and should've married someone else—in his own race? She owed him the truth. "You are the most responsible person I know, and you take your religion seriously. You may not even realize it, but this is about a sense of duty—Michael Clark doing the right thing despite the inevitable outcome."

His mouth fell open. "Is that what you think?" He shook his head. "I'm on my knees asking you to believe me. I fell in love with you that first day in the doctors' lounge when you spilled coffee on your hand."

"I don't know."

He stood and paced the room. "Are you now doubtful about our relationship because I'm black?" He stopped and stared down at her.

She pushed to her feet and stood near his side. "No, I don't see the color of your skin. I love you. I love Michael the man you are inside. But I don't know if you're being honest with yourself."

"If you could look inside my heart, you'd see the truth. But if you won't marry me, at least give our child a chance in this life. I want to adopt our baby after you give birth. If I can't have you, at least allow me the privilege of raising your child—and mine."

Tammy stood in stunned silence. How could he say that if he didn't love her? Maybe he really did. But Darnell's visit still weighed heavy on her mind. "No, Michael. I could never take your family away from you."

He furrowed his brow. "What are you talking about?"

"I know your father would disown you if you married me. Your mother would be deprived of her son forever." She ran a hand through her hair. "I could never do that to her or the rest of your family."

Michael shook his head. "Tammy, I have no idea where you got that idea." He gazed somewhere over her shoulder. "Wait a minute. Who told you my family would disown me?"

"Darnell was here tonight. He explained it all. I know much of what he said reflects his own opinions, but he had to acquire them from somewhere. Parents pass on their prejudices to their children. You can't deny that."

"He was here, in your apartment?" He clasped his fist into a tight ball.

"No, out front. We had a talk. He said your father was adamantly against mixed racial marriage and that he would disown you if we married. Your mother would never get to see you again or your child."

A growl gurgled up from Michael's throat. "That is absolutely not true. I'd like to punch him in the face right now. We were never taught as children to disrespect any other race. Darnell learned that garbage in college."

"You're saying your father would be happy to accept me as a daughter-in-law?"

"I … I'm not sure." Michael lowered his head. "He has questions about a mixed relationship. But now, I think since he's a Christian… "

Tammy folded her arms over her chest and turned her back to him. "Don't worry. I get the message." Darnell had told her the truth. Their father wasn't in favor of his sons marrying someone of another color and certainly wouldn't embrace the child from that union. Even if he didn't cut Michael off from the rest of the family, their association with his parents would be strained at best. "Your family would never accept me. I've made my decision, and it's the best for all of us. Me, you, and your family. After the abortion, I'll be out of your life."

Michael shook his head then swiped a hand over his mouth. "Tammy, you've got to reconsider."

"Please, Michael. This is hard for me. I need you to go now."

Tammy slowly walked to the entrance.

Michael stared at her, as if she'd change her mind. When he got to the door, he turned to face her, his face etched with emotion.

She dropped her gaze to the floor, unable to watch his painful expression any longer. After he walked out, she slowly pushed the door shut behind him. His final exit from her life ripped her heart out. Crumpling on the floor, she couldn't control the sobs that wracked her shoulders.

Chapter Twenty-Three

Tammy smoothed her scrubs top down over her pants and glanced around the living room for her car keys.

Nothing could erase the image of Michael's angst-ridden face as he left her apartment three days ago. A man wanting to adopt a baby. The gesture touched a place deep inside.

Were his words related to religious beliefs, or did he sincerely want to raise a child on his own? She couldn't imagine a busy single doctor responsible for a baby. But a greater obstacle was Michael's family who would shun a white woman's child. Hadn't Darnell made that clear?

She glanced at the clock in her kitchen. She still had a little time before she needed to leave for work. Time to call and make the appointment for the procedure. Her purse and keys sat on the bar between the living room and kitchen. Reaching down to the slot where she'd slipped the card, she pulled it out and keyed in the clinic phone number.

"El Camino Women's Health Center, Mrs. Moriarty speaking."

Just the person Tammy needed to talk to. "This is Tammy Crawford. I need to make an appointment." An empty feeling crept through the pit of her stomach. She hadn't expected it would be this hard.

"Yes, Ms. Crawford. I remember your case. How about a week from today at eleven in the morning? Would that work for you?"

Tammy forced the word out of her dry mouth. "Yes."

"Great. We have the results of your blood tests, and you're cleared for the procedure. Did we give you the information sheet on how to prepare?"

"Yes, wear comfortable clothes, no eating or drinking after midnight the night before, and bring a copy of my insurance."

"We'll discuss the type of anesthesia when you get here. And Ms. Crawford, you won't regret your decision."

How did she know? They'd only talked for ten minutes the day of the initial pregnancy test. Doubt still hung on like a persistent cough, but what else could she do?

"All right. I'll be there." Tammy clicked *off* and shoved the phone back. Hanging the purse straps on her shoulder, she picked up her keys and bolted out of the apartment, trying to ignore the dread and fear welling up inside. After next week, the pregnancy would be over. Is that what she truly wanted? But each time she questioned her decision, the same answer arose. What were the other options?

The next seven days would be the longest ever. But when it was over, life would go on like always. Right? She'd never make the mistake again of allowing her impulsive actions to dictate. Never again would she fall into bed with a guy until she was married.

Heaviness hung over her all the way to the hospital. The drive seemed endless. After she parked the car, she stepped into the elevator and punched *four*.

"Hey, we meet here again." A familiar voice greeted her.

Tammy glanced toward the back of the elevator. Once again, Glorilyn Neilson grinned at her. Why was it that every time Tammy felt the worst, Glorilyn seemed to show up? "Hey." Tammy attempted to muster a smile. "What are you up to today?"

"I'm off from school for Presidents' Week, so I'm heading up to the NICU. My favorite activity. Cuddling the babies." She peered at Tammy and touched her arm. "But I sense you're carrying a pretty heavy burden today. I can see it in your eyes."

How could Glorilyn know? The young woman's compassionate attention crashed through a wall she didn't want anyone to penetrate. Without her permission, tears formed. One renegade drop of moisture rolled down her cheek, and Tammy's cheeks burned. How could she allow her emotions to show like this?

When the bell dinged for the fourth floor, Glorilyn followed her off. "Look, Tammy. My heart goes out to anyone who's burdened. I have a feeling you haven't told too many people about this. Am I right?"

Uncanny. Tammy nodded and swiped away a drop of moisture.

Glorilyn peered at her with a gaze that threatened to evoke tears again. "Can we go somewhere to talk for a second? I know you've got to get to work."

The clock on the wall said ten minutes before her shift. Did she really want to reveal anything to Glorilyn? She shook her head. "No, I'm okay, really. Just tired."

"All right, then. But I'm going to pray for you, Nurse Crawford." Glorilyn smiled and walked toward the elevators.

As if Glorilyn was a nautical life preserver, Tammy couldn't let her float away. "Wait." She could at least get her opinion about abortion. Maybe all Christians didn't oppose it.

Glorilyn turned, a question on her face.

The family waiting area was deserted at the moment. "Let's go over there. I want to ask you something."

"Sure." Glorilyn's face brightened as they strolled toward the open room with a TV, comfortable vinyl chairs, and a coffee table.

No need to reveal that Tammy meant herself when she asked a supposedly generic question about the procedure. She stopped at the picture window at the end of the room with a view of city traffic below. "I ... I just want your opinion."

As if the question were written on her forehead, Glorilyn peered at Tammy. "I'll be happy to share my views if I can."

"I ... uh, have a friend who's in a jam." Tammy cleared her throat. "She's pregnant and is considering abortion. She's asked me my opinion, and I'm not sure what I believe. I'm not religious or anything like that. Are there times when abortion is okay?"

Did Glorilyn feel empathy toward Tammy's so-called friend? Glorilyn's eyes glowed like a flickering fireplace, and she smoothed her hand over Tammy's. "That tiny new life inside your friend is very precious to God. He can even see its little unformed frame. I don't think there's ever a right time to take the life of a child that God knit together inside your friend's body or anyone's for that matter."

Just as Tammy thought. Glorilyn embraced the pro-life posture. She'd never give Tammy the answer she wanted to hear. "All right, thanks. I've got to get to work now."

"Look." She rested her hand on Tammy's arm as if to restrain her. "I'd like to talk to your friend."

Taking in a deep breath didn't change the truth. There was no other person. "I'll be honest. She doesn't want to hear any Bible quotes or religious stuff."

"I understand." Glorilyn nodded. "I wasn't thinking about preaching to her. But I have a buddy from high school named Lori. I want your friend to hear her story. Could you arrange for her to meet us at your place tonight? Before she has the abortion."

No preaching? "I suppose. But I'm warning you, she'll walk out if you try to get all holy with her."

"I can guarantee she won't talk about religion." Glorilyn grinned. "Actually, Lori hasn't given her life to the Lord yet." She continued to gaze at Tammy. "What's your acquaintance's name?" she whispered.

Tammy cast her gaze to her shoes then back to Glorilyn's pretty face with her bright eyes and upturned nose. "You know her name already." Tammy scribbled her address on a slip of paper and wrapped Glorilyn's fingers around it.

"I'll see you tonight." Glorilyn squeezed her hand. "Seven okay?"

"Fine." Why had she disclosed her secret? Somehow she trusted the young woman with her silence. Tammy stiffened into a rigid block of cement. Perhaps the decision to hear out what Lori had to say wasn't a good one. But at least she wouldn't expound on some religious philosophy.

*****

Tammy paced the room and glanced at the wall clock. Ten minutes until seven. She still questioned the decision to listen to this woman's story, but she couldn't change her mind now. Glorilyn and Lori would be here in minutes.

After several more turns around her living room, she attempted to quiet her churning thoughts and anxieties. She relaxed into her side chair across from the couch. Only moments later, the bell rang.

With icy hands and not knowing what to expect, Tammy turned the knob and opened the door.

Glorilyn stood next to a lovely young woman with long, dark hair cascading to her shoulders.

"Come in." She stepped back from the threshold.

"Lori, this is Tammy, Joella's sister." Glorilyn smiled. "Tammy, my friend Lori."

Lori gave her a warm smile. "Glorilyn's told me you're a geriatrics nurse. That's awesome. I'm studying to be an RN as well."

A bit of tension released when she gazed at the friendly young woman. She pointed to the couch. "Please sit down."

As if both women felt at home, they eased down on the couch and glanced around the apartment. "Your home is beautiful," Glorilyn said.

Tammy sat back in the chair. "Thank you." She turned to Lori. "So how many more years do you have to finish?"

"Just one after this." She beamed. "I hope to do my training at El Camino General in the ER."

"You're a brave woman." Tammy chuckled. "It takes a special skill to practice nursing in that unpredictable environment." She liked Glorilyn's friend already. Maybe because of their mutual interest in nursing. "Can I get you anything to drink?" This wasn't a social call, but it didn't hurt to show a little hospitality.

"Not for me, thanks," Glorilyn said.

Lori smiled. "Me either, Tammy, but I appreciate it."

"I want to thank you for allowing us to come by tonight." Glorilyn set her keys down on the coffee table and glanced at Tammy. "Lori's shared with me that her story is tough to tell, so I'd like to thank you, too, Lori." She squeezed Lori's hand. "But I think what you have to say is something Tammy might want to hear."

"Though it's painful," Lori shifted on the couch next to Glorilyn, "I'm grateful for the opportunity to tell my story."

Pain. Obviously she didn't mean physical pain.

Lori peered at Tammy. "Glorilyn tells me you have a friend —"

"No, I might as well set things straight." She looked at Glorilyn. "I'm sure she figured it out. There is no friend." She gulped with the words. Other than the health clinic director and Michael, no one knew of her pregnancy until now. "I'm a little over six weeks pregnant and have an appointment for an abortion next week." Saying the words made her more uncomfortable than those times when Joella preached at her.

Though Tammy expected Glorilyn to gasp or give a look of horror, JD's sister only watched her with compassion.

Lori folded her hands in her lap, never taking her gaze from Tammy. "As you'll see from my story, I was once in your shoes. I want to share what happened in hopes that it helps you with the decision."

"Glorilyn promised you wouldn't push conservative Christian views on me."

"You can be assured of that. Even today I'm not a believer like Glorilyn is." She turned and smiled at her friend. "Though Glorilyn still tries to get me to go to church. One day, I'll take her up on it."

At least Lori's story wouldn't be influenced by Christian doctrine. "I'm interested in your point of view."

"I used to not believe in God at all. Since my abortion, I've begun to suspect there is a divine being Who created our vast world. Right now, He's a vague entity. I don't have the faith Glorilyn keeps talking about."

Glorilyn smiled. "That's okay, my friend. I'm praying for you."

"I've come to believe there is a God," Tammy could barely voice the truth, "but it's like that for me, too. He's somewhere out in the universe, but I don't know Him personally like my sister, Joella, claims she does."

"Then let me continue." Lori grasped a tissue from her purse and peered at Tammy, her smile fading.

Pulling her legs up under her, Tammy leaned back in the chair.

"Right after I graduated from high school at the age of eighteen, I found myself pregnant." Lori took a breath. "My boyfriend said he had no interest in getting married and gave me money to get an abortion. I hadn't told my parents." She twisted the tissue in her hands. "My father would've killed me, and my mother might've had a heart attack."

Talk of parents saddened Tammy. "At least you had a mother

and father. My mom died last year, and my dad ran off to Europe."

Lori frowned. "I'm sorry. That must be hard. I'm glad we're having this chat since you don't have parents to talk with. Knowing what I know today, I regret not sharing my problem with them."

Tammy peered at Glorilyn. "Nevertheless, I'd like both of you to keep this in confidence. Joella has no idea."

"I should've reminded you from the start." Glorilyn stood and hugged Tammy. "What we talk about this evening won't leave this room. Lori doesn't discuss her story with many people either."

Lori nodded. "I suppose you're the third person I've told besides my friend who took me to the appointment. Glorilyn was one, and the other was a young woman, like you, contemplating abortion." She shifted on the couch. "But let me continue. I had no one to advise me about what to do, so I took my boyfriend's money and made an appointment at the women's health clinic. The same place I assume you have your appointment."

"Yes." Tammy glanced at her lap. Somehow she couldn't meet Lori's gaze.

"That day ... the day of the appointment, Jane, my friend from high school, drove me there. When I walked into the clinic, the waiting room was full of young women. Not one seemed happy to be there. I looked around at the girls and told myself I wasn't like the others. I was different, but then I'd landed in the same predicament they had. After forty-five minutes someone called my name. I could hardly follow the woman, I felt so scared and nervous." Lori wiped her eyes with the tissue. "The nurse who wasn't even wearing scrubs took me into a room not much bigger than a storage closet. The walls were painted an ugly green and the counters a bleak gray. In the middle of the room, a hard stainless-steel table occupied most of the space. The nurse said to sit on the edge and wait."

Tammy shifted and reached for a tissue. The story was difficult to hear. It must've been tough on Lori then and again today to relive the memories.

"After what seemed like an hour, a doctor in a white lab jacket came in," Lori continued. "He never smiled. He thrust a sheet of paper at me with drawings and diagrams of what he was about to do. Then he handed me a clip board with a release form and asked me to sign. He said he couldn't go ahead with the procedure until I paid him the money. I took the cash from my purse and passed it to him. Today I suppose the financial arrangements are made with the one of the receptionists.

"Finally, he told me to get undressed and handed me a sheet. 'Cover up,' he'd said then left the room. As if that would hide my body from him. I undressed then laid on the cold, uncomfortable table, still in shock over where life had taken me. At last, the nurse returned to see if I was ready. After a few minutes, the doctor began the process. I'm not sure there was medication in the shot he gave me because the pain was unbearable. I cried out, and the doctor yelled at me. He told me if I didn't be quiet, he wouldn't finish the procedure."

Tears rolled down Tammy's eyes. Her training had always taught her to show compassion for a patient, not disdain. "The doctor had no right to treat you that way."

"Nevertheless, that's what happened. Only the nurse showed compassion. She held my hand and told me it was almost over. Perhaps that's why I decided to become an RN. Her touch meant so much that day." Lori took a deep breath. "All I could do now was stare at the ceiling, count the squares, and beg God to forgive me. I couldn't imagine how my life would change. I kept asking if I could forgive myself for what I had allowed to happen to my body. I jerked again with pain, but the doctor continued as if he couldn't care less what I felt. Looking back now, I can't tell you how long it took, but finally the doctor rose from the stool where he sat and glared at me. His only words were 'Take the pill next time.' I made up a story and told him I'd been raped, and he shrugged and walked out of the room. In pain, I struggled to get dressed and stumbled out to the waiting room to meet Jane, my friend who'd accompanied me. Since my parents were out of town, I spent the next few days in silence, enduring the physical and mental hurt." Lori put her hands over her face, her shoulders shaking.

Glorilyn slipped her arms around her friend and closed her eyes. "I'm so sorry. I know the memory is hard to bear." Glorilyn's lips moved as she held Lori until the sobs subsided.

Finally Lori looked up. "Retelling the story impacted me more than ever today. Somehow it was as if I went through the abortion again."

Lori had made a great sacrifice to share her experience.

Tammy rose and ran her hand down the young woman's shoulder. "I can't thank you enough for risking the pain again."

"There's more." Lori looked up at her with a tear-stained face.

Tammy frowned and returned to her chair. What else could happen after that horrendous experience? She peered at Lori.

"After that day, my life was never the same. I will always remember the cold, hard table and the nasty green walls. Honestly I've never been able to reconcile my guilt about that day or to feel forgiven by God for paying a doctor to kill my child." She turned to Glorilyn. "My friend here tells me if I knew God better, I could find His forgiveness. I'm considering it."

"I hope Lori's story has helped you, Tammy." Glorilyn pressed her palms together. "And I was true to my word. She didn't preach at you or quote scripture. She only described what happened."

"I never would've imagined an abortion could be that traumatic, especially afterwards." Tammy shook her head. "You've given me something to think about."

The two women stood and began to gather their things. Glorilyn turned to Tammy. "If you have any more questions, please let us know."

"I will. Thank you both for coming tonight." Tammy hugged each and then Glorilyn and Lori walked out into the hall.

Lori's account of her abortion impacted Tammy. If nothing else, it brought a renewed desire to show compassion to all patients, but the story also prompted her to consider once again her decision.

Tammy gently shut the door and rested her weary body against it. Lori's words echoed in her mind. "I've never been able to reconcile my guilt."

Why would Lori feel guilty over a mere procedure? People didn't feel remorse when having a gall bladder removed or an appendix.

Seeing the so called "product of conception" for herself might shed light. Tammy marched over to her desk and switched on her computer.

She plopped down in front of the laptop and googled *picture of fetus at six weeks.* Though she'd looked at other images in nursing school, she had to witness it for herself again tonight.

Many of the photos were illustrations, but when she scrolled down a little farther, she gasped. The next picture showed an actual miscarriage at six weeks. Little feet and hands were shaped like paddles. The beginnings of small eyes were evident on the tiny round head. Though not completely formed, the fetus looked like a miniature baby.

Tammy paced the living room, pressing her hands against both sides of her head. What should she believe? What she saw looked like a baby, but did God consider it a human at this point in fetal development?

*****

Tammy adjusted the stethoscope around her neck and stepped into Mrs. Tyson's room. Pneumonia. So many of the patients recently seemed to suffer from the infection that impaired lung function. The flu virus complicated Mrs. Tyson's case.

The chart hanging at the end of the bed reminded her. Yesterday, a chest X-ray and blood test had confirmed the disease. Today, she'd need a CT scan.

The eighty-year-old slowly opened her eyes. "Good morning." She hacked a dry cough. "Can you see there on my chart? When will the doctor let me go home?" She coughed again.

"Good morning, Mrs. Tyson. We don't know quite yet. It all depends on how your body responds to the antibiotics. Soon I hope."

"I can't wait until I can get back to my grandkids. And my doggie. I miss them."

"I understand." Tammy adjusted the IV. "I bet your grandchildren love you a lot."

The elderly woman turned her head to the side and gazed up with watery brown eyes. "I'm blessed to have such a loving family. How about you, dear? Do you have kids?"

Pain as real as a slap in the face impacted Tammy. The sweet woman had no idea of the implications of her question. "No, I'm not married."

She patted Tammy's hand. "Well, I know that special man will come along someday."

Why did people of Mrs. Tyson's generation think that the only answer to happiness was to get married and have kids? Yet was the notion all that bad when you loved someone like the way she felt about Michael? Why did her life seem so complicated? She felt like a small, insignificant rowboat in an immense ocean tossed here and there.

Tammy smiled at the lady and listened to her chest, the persistent wheezing audible. She jotted down several notations on the woman's chart. "I'll be back later to check on you." She pointed to the railing on the side of the bed. "Here's the nurse call button if you need anything."

"Thank you, young lady."

"You're certainly welcome." Tammy slipped out of the room and glanced at her watch. Time for a break. A good thing because she couldn't concentrate on anything but the impending appointment in four days. Maybe she shouldn't have listened to Lori's story. It only served to add doubt to her already confused mental state.

If she could just get off the floor for a few minutes, maybe she'd perk up. An image of the hospital gardens where she'd walked with Michael a while back drew her. Though it was a cold February day, the sun shone brightly. She grabbed her coat and took the elevator to the main floor.

Walking out the side door to the hospital grounds felt like stepping into another world. The brisk, fresh air filled her lungs as she breathed deeply and set out on the trail. Increasing her pace, she moved toward the covered gazebo and to the bench where she and Michael had embraced.

"Tammy, wait up."

Her heart pumped harder in her chest as the masculine voice she knew so well called, his breathy tone sounding urgent.

Michael. Seeing him would be difficult, but she couldn't avoid him now. She spun around and peered at the man in a lab jacket rushing toward her. Surprising he didn't wear an overcoat.

"I saw you from my office window. I have to talk to you."

She took a step closer. "Aren't you cold?"

He shrugged. "I left a pile of work on my desk and headed straight to the elevator. Tammy, I can barely concentrate. Please tell me you haven't gone in for the— "

"Michael, I've given this so much thought. There's no other answer. Your family would never accept me or our child." She tossed a strand of hair from her face. "What else am I supposed to do? You said you'd adopt the baby, but what kind of a life would you have then? Whether we were married or not, your family would refuse to embrace their grandchild, and my parents are gone. Darnell would despise his nephew or niece. Our lives would be miserable."

"My mother would never object."

"Yeah, but there's still the matter of your father."

He scrubbed a hand over his mouth. "With God's help, we'd overcome those problems. We'd live our lives with or without his blessings."

"That's another thing." Her words were shrill. "I believe in God, but I'm not as sold out to church traditions the way you are. You'd begin to resent me one day."

He hung his head and mumbled. "If I denied it, would you believe me?"

"I want to, but I can't. If I had your faith …" Tammy gazed at the gazebo and sighed. "My appointment is next Monday at eleven."

Gripping her hands, he squeezed. "I wish there was something I could say to dissuade you. My life will never be the same again. Can't you understand that?"

Michael's words seemed a little over the top. Surely he didn't actually mean them. He'd move on in a month or two, just as she would.

Hot tears rolled down her face, and she turned, her feet ferrying her back to the hospital as fast as she could go. "I can't. I just can't see things your way."

Chapter Twenty-Four

Tammy dangled her feet off the edge of the table, her body covered only by a rough-textured, white sheet. Since she'd driven herself to the clinic, she'd decided to get a cab home and pick up her car later. No one else besides Michael could know she was here or why.

The stainless-steel examination table didn't seem quite as hard as Lori described. Papers signed and the fees met, Tammy's stomach whirled like a hurricane threatening destruction. Would her experience be any different than the young nursing student's? Gritting her teeth, she braced for the pain to come in only moments.

Repeating over and over Mrs. Moriarty's words kept her sitting on the table, though part of her wanted to flee. *A heartbeat didn't make the fetus a breathing, thinking person.*

She glanced at the wall clock. Ten thirty. Since they called and asked her to come in an hour earlier, she should be finished by a little after eleven.

Like Lori described, the nurse spoke with a soft, reassuring tone. She patted Tammy's shoulder then turned to the shiny gray side table, readying the instruments that would soon remove the fetus, no different than getting rid of a piece of tissue within the body, similar to a biopsy. "Don't worry, dear, the doctor is only taking out the product of conception. You'll have a pain block and will experience a minimum of discomfort."

A notion seeped into her brain then her soul then her heart like osmosis. Would the product of conception, as the nurse described it, feel anything? She'd read that beginning at eight weeks, a fetus could experience pain. How could a blob of tissue feel anything if it weren't alive and a real person? Images of the picture she'd seen online of the miscarriage at six weeks flashed in her brain, torturing her. The tiny limbs, the eye sockets—

Covering her face with her hands didn't erase what was already in her mind.

What were the answers? She couldn't be sure of anything. Once again, she shook off the notion and glanced around the room at the same green walls and gray counters Lori talked about. Maybe she shouldn't have listened to Glorilyn and Lori. Maybe she made more of the pictures on the internet than she should—and the stray words from the Bible that still whispered to her. A baby would be a great inconvenience, she reminded herself for the hundredth time. She was a career woman after all.

Now a swirl of reflections barraged her mind. One after another. Almost as if one thought warred with the other. Pulling and tugging. She couldn't control her racing thoughts.

A scene from childhood seeped into her brain. An eight-year-old Tammy sat in the Sunday school room of a church where her parents used to take her and Joella. Five other children gathered around a rectangular table. A white haired woman that Tammy had wished was her grandmother pointed to a felt board with little cutouts of the Ten Commandments from the Bible. "And number six, children, says 'You shall not commit murder.' What does murder mean?"

A little boy next to Tammy raised his hand. "That means to kill something, like I shouldn't take anybody's life."

You shall not commit murder. You shall not commit murder.

The words she'd learned reverberated over and over in Tammy's mind, like they'd done before. If the product of conception was a living person, she'd be committing murder. But what were the odds? If there was any chance that Joella was correct, how could Tammy take the risk?

If.

A deep sigh overflowed from the clamor tossing within.

A heartbeat didn't make the fetus a breathing, thinking person. Mrs. Moriarty's message blared.

That tiny new life inside your friend is very precious to God. He can even see its little unformed body. Once again, Glorilyn's words rushed over her—against her will.

If Tammy went through with the procedure, she'd possibly destroy the life of a person God valued and knew. If it was a person.

The doctor entered the room. "All right, Ms. Crawford, we're ready to begin." With gloved hands, he filled a syringe, tapping it several times to remove air bubbles. He walked toward her. "You shouldn't feel any pain with the numbing medication."

The nurse held out a paper cup with a tablet and another with water. "Valium will help you relax."

*****

Michael straightened and looked down at the new life in the incubator. *Thank You, Lord. This baby stands a good chance of survival.*

A surge of anxiety pummeled him like blows to his chest. He jerked his gaze up to the wall clock. Ten forty.

With an exasperated huff of air, he yanked his stethoscope from around his neck and shoved it in his pocket. He could no longer concentrate. For the welfare of his young patients, he had to leave the floor. Rushing toward Charlotte at the nurses' desk, he glanced at her. "I've got an emergency. Call Dr. Valentine if you need him. NP Robson is here."

Charlotte lifted her brows. "I'm sorry, Dr. Clark. I'll certainly be praying."

He ran a quick hand over his mouth and raced to the elevators. The women's clinic was ten blocks away. If necessary, he'd kidnap Tammy and remove her from the waiting room. Sure the cops might arrest him, but if he could save the baby, it would all be worth it.

He punched *down* when he got to the elevator then stepped inside when the doors slid open. Who was he kidding? He couldn't violate Tammy's choice. But he'd implore her there in the middle of the clinic to listen to him.

Making his way to his parking space, he revved up the engine and pulled out of the hospital. He took the next street to the right and sped through an amber light. *Careful, Clark. If you get stopped, you won't reach her in time.*

The streets were busy, and Michael had to slow. He pounded the steering wheel. "God, please let me get there before it's too late."

Tightness in his chest squeezed. Horns blared and a taxi driver signaled with his middle finger out the window of the yellow sedan. Michael gripped both sides of his head. "God, this can't be happening."

He dared a glance at the car's clock. "Dear Lord, it's ten forty-five." Unless God divinely intervened, the procedure would begin soon, and it would be too late.

Feeling helpless and out of control, Michael's stomach tightened with frustration. "Oh, God. Save my child."

When the traffic finally started moving, he dared another look at the digital clock. Eleven o'clock. The procedure had probably already begun. He hadn't reached the clinic in time.

He pulled into the health center's parking lot and shoved the driver's door open. With legs that seemed constrained by heavy hand weights, he stepped out the car. With all the force he could muster, he rushed through the front door of the clinic.

*****

Questions warred in Tammy's mind. She lay prone on the hard surface, her feet in stirrups, the second time she'd had to assume the position. Maybe she should've left twenty minutes ago when the procedure was delayed, but some force paralyzed her, kept her frozen on the hard table.

In all her nursing career, she'd never misplaced an instrument. Though a kindly woman, the clinic nurse postponed the procedure when she couldn't find the uterine curette.

With a huff and the shake of his head, the doctor stepped toward the end of the metal table. "Are we finally ready, Ms. Capshaw?"

The red-faced woman nodded. "Again, I apologize, Doctor. Somehow the instrument wound up in the room down the hall."

The pointed end of the needle in the doctor's hand inched toward her.

Before I formed you in the womb, I knew you.

She gasped. The words echoed over and over in her mind. A strong impression spoke to her soul, as if Someone pleaded with her not to kill the life within. The communication didn't condemn, only implored her. The strong impression of peace remained.

"No." She screamed, pushing away the paper cup the nurse offered. Tammy propelled from the table.

Placing a protective hand around her abdomen, she rushed out of the room, not daring to look at the doctor's expression or the questioning stare the nurse probably wore on her face.

As if chased by a hoard of devils, she rushed into the dressing room and twisted the tiny key in the slot on the locker. She quickly lifted the lever and grabbed her clothes. Dressing at a furious speed, she snatched her purse and raced out the back door.

As she sat down into the driver's seat and started the engine, she closed her eyes and took a breath. Why did it take so long to sink in? She caressed the protrusion below her waistband. The baby was real, and she'd be destroying a life if she went through with it. Michael's words were true when he said God knew the baby even before He formed it.

Glorilyn said God could see the little unformed body. Though these thoughts had nudged her before, this time the words *you shall not commit murder* bellowed at her. Patting her stomach, she exhaled. "Okay, little baby, it's just you and me now. We're in this for better or for worse."

JUNE FOSTER

Chapter Twenty-Five

Shortly after eleven, Michael walked in the front door of El Camino's Women's' Health Center, his heart heavy. Why bother rushing now? He could no longer stop the abortion. At least he could offer Tammy a ride home when she finished, though seeing her in pain and knowing what had happened would be hard.

He resented her choice to take the baby's life, yet he still loved her. Just because someone deeply disappointed you didn't mean you abandoned them. Regardless, he prayed for the Lord to heal her life and use her guilt for His glory, the guilt that would invariably materialize now.

A clerk at the front desk filed a manila folder in a metal cabinet and turned to him. "Yes, may I help you?"

"Tammy Crawford? She had an appointment at eleven. I'd like to speak with her when she comes out."

The clerk wrinkled her brow and gave him a quizzical look. "I'm not free to talk about any patient's case, but I can tell you all the morning appointments have come and gone."

Michael tapped his head. Of course the receptionist wasn't going to give him any information because of HIPPA laws. "All right, thank you."

Tammy gone? How could that be? Even if the abortion had started earlier, they didn't give her the usual recuperation time.

As if Michael stumbled through a dark room unsure of his steps, he trudged back to his car. But he knew what he had to do. Though seeing Tammy might be the hardest thing he'd ever done, he had to check on her.

If he didn't have God's strength, he'd never be able to maintain sanity. His hope in the Lord—the only anchor in his life right now.

He started the engine, but grief paralyzed him. His child had died today. Slowly, his shoulders began to shake. Covering his face, he couldn't stop the tears that leaked from his eyes and down his cheeks and onto his neck. His sobs sounded foreign to his ears. He seldom allowed this kind of emotion, but now, sorrow overwhelmed him.

Though it would be easy to blame or resent Tammy, he chose to channel his growing anger in a different direction. On a society that accepted the killing of innocent lives. People were deceived. Sacrificing children because of their so called inconvenience.

For the second time, Michael pounded the steering wheel. If he wasn't careful, he'd knock it off the shaft. "God, I long for Your righteousness," he bellowed. "Open hearts and minds to the atrocity of abortion."

Instead of heading back to the hospital, he turned toward Tammy's neighborhood. Emotion threatened again, but Michael bit his tongue until it hurt. He needed to man-up and face her now. Finally arriving in her neighborhood, he pulled up in front of her apartment house.

The slow climb to the second floor seemed to take two hours. What would he say to her? What condition would she be in after no recuperation time? With a cold finger, he pressed her door bell and waited.

The door squeaked open a few inches and a bright-eyed Tammy gazed back at him. More animated than he'd seen her in a month. Surely the abortion hadn't produced this positive reaction. "Michael? What are you doing here?"

More curious now than anything, he peered at her. "Are you okay? May I come in?"

She nodded and opened the door wider. A loose-fitting T-shirt draped over her jeans.

Glancing down at her as he walked over the threshold, he examined her from top to bottom. She didn't appear to be in pain, but then he wasn't sure. "I went to the clinic, and they said all the morning patients had gone home. How did you manage to get here? The clinic personnel didn't even give you time to rest?"

Inside the living room, Tammy faced him, rubbing her hand over her abdomen. "I thought long and hard, Michael. It finally came to me." She paced toward the kitchen and back again. "Please sit down."

Michael slowly dropped onto the couch and gazed at Tammy who'd sat in the chair across from him. He couldn't imagine what she would tell him.

She took a deep breath. "The doctor was ready to give me the paracervical block. I stared at the point of the menacing syringe he thrust toward me. The nurse offered a valium tablet, to make me relax. But I knew." She covered her face with both hands. "I knew that afterwards ..." Her shoulders shook. "Nothing would take away the guilt. But more importantly, I figured it out. What I was going to do was wrong." She swallowed a sob. Once again she swept a protective hand over her abdomen. "It's okay. Our baby is still safely inside."

His mouth fell slack. Hearing her words yet not totally perceiving their meaning, he filled his lungs with a deep gasp of air. "What? Say that again?"

Tears formed in her eyes. "Our child—he's right here." She patted her stomach. "Somehow I began to understand the truth. I couldn't take the life of an innocent life." She sat down next to him. "Forgive me, for what I almost did—murdering our unborn baby." Her breath caught with wretched moans. "I'm so sorry. I didn't consider you either. This child is half yours, and I disregarded your feelings as a father."

Though unable to fully understand, Michael comprehended that their child still existed. He or she would have a chance at life no matter what. Overwhelming relief surged over him. His baby had been resurrected from the dead. "Thank you, Lord. Thank you, Lord." He slipped his hand over hers. "What happened? How were you able to change your mind?"

Tammy leaned over, her shoulders hunched. "I had so much advice, Michael. Joella described her six-week pregnancy as a tiny baby. You told me again and again that it wasn't a blob of tissue but a child. A young nursing student even shared her horrendous experience in the abortion clinic. But I didn't want to listen."

"Then what?" Michael caught his breath, taking in shallow gulps of air. He could barely grasp the meaning of her words.

"What finally made the difference today?"

As if reliving the incident, Tammy sat up straight and wiped tears from her cheeks. Her blank gaze seemed to focus on nothing. "I stared at the ugly green walls in the abortion clinic. For months, scriptures I'd learned as a child had echoed in my brain, but I ignored them. When I sat on the hard table, I remembered a Sunday school lesson. Back then, I believed every word my teacher said. Once again, the words impressed me as true. At first, I tried to put the vision out of my mind, but I couldn't."

Michael's mouth fell open. "What? I didn't know you went to Sunday school as a girl."

"For awhile, yes. My parents took Joella and me. I suppose that was a more settled time in my life. After that Joella continued on in the faith, but I resisted."

"Why? Because girls with red hair are rebellious?" He gave a low chuckle.

She grinned then her smile faded. "Today I heard words I'd learned long ago. They echoed to me from the past."

"What words?"

"I heard my Sunday school teacher repeating *do not commit murder*. Not just once but over and over." She dabbed a tissue under her eye. "Nothing made a difference until that message blared at me. I knew the chances were good the fetal material was a baby. Even if unformed. I couldn't do it, Michael. I couldn't take that chance." She rubbed her stomach. "Not if this is a real baby."

More grateful than he'd ever been in his life, Michael sat next to Tammy and lifted one hand in the air. He closed his eyes. "Thank you, Jesus. You saved this little one's life."

Tammy peered at him. "You came to check on me ... even when you thought ... "

"I've told you all along, and you wouldn't believe me. I love you." He smoothed his hand over hers again and held on. Their child was alive.

Lifting his arm, he slid it around Tammy.

Sighing deeply, she nestled into the circle of his embrace.

Weary from the tension, he closed his eyes and thanked God again. After a while, he opened them.

Out the window, the wind whipped the bushes and trees, tossing the branches back and forth. The gray sky darkened a shade and finally large snowflakes began to fall to the ground. Something that didn't happen every winter in El Camino.

Tammy's silky hair and petite shoulders felt light against him. If she allowed God's word to speak to her at the clinic, perhaps the Lord was drawing her to Himself. He swallowed hard. Maybe someday she'd trust in Him as Michael had prayed for weeks. "Tammy, I still want very much for us to have a future together."

She sat up, and Michael missed the warmth in the crook of his arm. "I believe you love me, but there are still so many obstacles. I would be the one white woman at the family celebrations. How would they treat me?"

"I can't imagine how my mother could turn away from you or her little grandchild. If the way she dotes on Alexus's children is any indication."

"I assume Alexus is married to an African-American. In which case, her children are one hundred percent black."

"Yes, her husband is African-American. But what difference does that make?"

"Our child is half white. How would your father feel about that?"

"My dad recently gave his life to the Lord. Most of the time, people change their way of thinking when they become a Christian."

"Even about a matter as personal as his son's marriage to a white woman?"

"Listen, Tammy." Michael lifted her chin. "Even if my father didn't endorse our marriage completely, he'd never turn away from his flesh and blood. Darnell lied to you. I tried to tell you." He pulled her back into his arms. "I meant what I said when I asked you to marry me. Reconsider?"

"I do love you, Michael." She squeezed his hand. "But I still have doubts. I'm not sure I can trust in God like you do."

Michael blew out a breath. "We'll work it out."

"I can't, Michael."

*****

Tammy closed the door behind a saddened Michael, his shoulders slumped as he exited her apartment. She'd put him through so much, but how could she make a life with him? She couldn't force herself to embrace his deeply held beliefs.

She'd never be sorry now for her choice to carry the baby. Allowing things to go as far as the abortion clinic distressed her. She shuddered. How close she'd come to killing her child and how greatly she regretted it. Would God forgive her?

Somehow she'd figure out a way to go to school during pregnancy. Then afterwards... A specific plan hadn't materialized, but she still had seven more months to figure things out.

An image of the wide-eyed Michael when she said she couldn't marry him sent an ache to her chest. She wasn't as demonstrative in her meager faith in a Supreme Being as Michael. God felt distant and foreign. Michael acted like God was his best friend.

What if they were married and she did something that didn't meet with his Christian standards? Or what if she allowed a curse word to escape? Maybe Michael would make her go to church with him every week, and she wasn't ready. No, marriage wouldn't work.

Chapter Twenty-Six

With temps in the sixties, the balmy March day held the promise of spring. Tammy parked in the lot at Lower Ormond Park and paused, allowing the silence to surround her. For days a myriad of thoughts hadn't allowed rest. Something had changed. Never before had she felt incomplete, as if keenly aware that life held more than she'd allowed into her world. Like setting out down a path but colliding with a fence, unable to journey farther. Where had these foreign thoughts originated?

Exiting the car, she walked toward the trail head, hoping she wouldn't run into a fence down the way. Crazy. There were no barriers in the park she'd hiked many times. With any luck, the fresh air and dazzling sunshine would clear her thinking.

After a fourth of a mile, the rippling waters of Big Lunas Creek came into view. How many times had Mom and Dad told her and Joella about the spot where they fell in love? The park and the creek permitted her to feel a little closer to her absent parents, a mother she'd never see again, and a father who'd disappeared from her life.

Breathing clean air deeply into her lungs, she followed the path that led along the gentle flow of the water. Tiny buds had begun to form on leafless trees. In one spot, a tangle of vine growth formed a canopy over the creek. Would this place hold the answers she needed?

A cement table came into view at the next bend of the river. Tammy eased down on the bench, drawing her tennis shoe-clad feet up on the seat. The twill and tweet of a bird in the tree overhead serenaded her.

All her life, she'd fled from opinions others tried to force on her. Joella preached about religion for years, and Tammy had always rejected her views. Even when Michael encouraged her to know God better, she recoiled at the idea. Why?

Tammy rested her head on her knees. A gentle breeze caught a strand of hair on her forehead and lifted it. As if a neon sign flashed in front of her closed eyes, she visualized one word. *Pride.* Her skin prickled as the notion slapped her in the face, yet oddly enough, condemnation hadn't accompanied the thought.

Pride. All her life she wanted to do things her way, never considering other alternatives.

The river gave a little gurgling sound as it flowed over river rocks. A sense of hunger overwhelmed her. Not for food, but something else. What, she couldn't be sure. But a gnawing ache filled her soul.

Opening her eyes, she gazed at the new growth around her. A profusion of wild flowers popping up amidst the dry grass, a bird carrying a twig to her nest. Though in high school she'd learned that the earth began spontaneously with a big bang, what or who instigated the phenomenon and provided the materials for the occurrence? So many questions and never any clear-cut answers.

As if a glass of cold water quenched her thirst, she began to understand. The deepest desire of her heart was to know God. No longer would she settle for the image of a distant and foreign deity. But what had stood in the way all these years? Pride had come between her and the Maker of the universe.

A powerful tingle ran down her spine. Someone out there bigger than she ran the universe. A door began to open that had been shut for too many years.

She continued to stroll down the path, joyfulness surging inside, lightening her step. Joella. She'd always respected her sister but thought she was ill informed. Why hadn't she paid more attention to the change in JD after he left the cult where he grew up and embraced Joella's beliefs?

Even the contrast between two brothers, Michael and Darnell, was telling. Michael, thoughtfully looking out for the needs of others. Had his faith set him apart from his prejudiced brother?

Reaching down to the clear, chilly river of the Big Lunas, she couldn't resist splashing water in her face. She needed to be clean, set free from the pride that swallowed her. She had to know God personally, like Joella and Michael.

*****

Memories of yesterday still warmed Tammy's heart, but nothing had taken away the longing. Though she had no idea how to connect with God now, the day of the abortion she'd felt His presence—and His voice.

The yearning persisted as she left the nurses' station to check on Mrs. Borden.

Sure she could talk to Joella, but she might say I told you so. Did Tammy want to approach Michael? What would he think? Maybe he'd finally lost patience with her. She smoothed her scrubs pants down, now fitting a bit tighter around her waist. She stepped into the patient's room.

"Good morning, Ms. Crawford. I was hoping I'd see you again. They told me yesterday was your day off." The white-haired woman's wrinkles lined her round face.

Tammy smiled. "It was. I decided to get some fresh air and took a walk in the Lower Ormond."

"I'm so envious, dear. I used to love hiking in the out-of-doors when I was younger." Mrs. Borden stared at Tammy, allowing her gaze to drop to her middle. "It seems youth has passed me by. But I still enjoy spending time on my back deck listening to the birds sing."

"Yes, ma'am. Yesterday in the park, they sounded like the California Symphony Choral Ensemble."

Mrs. Borden peered at Tammy's waist then up to her face. "Dear, I've always prided myself in knowing when a woman is expecting the birth of a new little one. Am I right?" Her eyes twinkled with mirth.

Heat filled Tammy's face. Was her condition actually evident already? She grinned at the woman. "You're very perceptive."

Like it or not, Tammy needed to face the truth. Others would know soon as well.

Chapter Twenty-Seven

Michael furiously hacked at the last couple of dandelions that invaded his front flower garden, but for almost two weeks, hard work hadn't quelled his disappointment in Tammy's choice not to marry him. Working outside in the yard usually relieved stress, but not this time.

A few of the unwanted plants he pulled up by the roots and wished he could weed out the regret that he and Tammy wouldn't raise their child as husband and wife. Prayer had occupied most of his free time lately, the only Source sustaining him. At least the chances he'd be able to get partial custody of their child were excellent.

Michael whipped off his cap and wiped the sweat from his forehead then plopped the hat back down. Thank God for a day off. He wouldn't even have to worry about going into the hospital. Jeff covered the NICU today.

The next step. Fertilizing the soil. He pushed the wheelbarrow around to the garage. Zipping open the top of the large plastic bag, he dumped half of the contents into the carrier. He hoisted the rolling cart up by the handles and proceeded to the garden. Soil finally tilled, he dumped a load of topsoil and raked it into the ground.

A car motor in front of the house caught his attention. He shaded his eyes and glanced toward the street. Then his breath caught in his throat.

*****

Taking a chance Michael would be at home, Tammy stopped her car in front of his condo. Saturday morning. Hopefully he had the day off.

Though she had no right to burden him again, she couldn't wait any longer to talk to him. Even if he'd lost patience and completely written her off, which she would've done weeks ago if it were her, maybe he'd answer a few questions. During the last months, he'd demonstrated deep faith in God, and she could no longer ignore her hunger to know more.

With her pulse hammering in her veins, she peered at the front of the house. Muscles flexing under a tattered T shirt, Michael tossed and raked soil in the flower garden with powerful swipes. Her heart seesawed with her wavering courage. He didn't appear to be in any mood to talk to her.

Gripping the rake, he looked up. For a second, he stared as if seeing an apparition. Then his mouth dropped open. Did she dare get out? She swallowed the apprehension and eased the car door open.

Michael stood motionless gazing at her, a frown between his brows. Then as if waking from a dream, he laid the rake down and brushed his hands together, knocking off the dirt.

Tammy tamped down the momentary urge to get back in the car and drive off, afraid of his rejection. She lifted her chin in an attempt to gain courage and pushed a smile in place. "Hello, Michael. I see you're busy, but do you have a moment to talk?"

He gave her a wary look. "Yeah, I could take a break from this. But I'm surprised to see you here."

"I know. I'm sorry to just drop by. I took a chance—"

"After you sent me on my way the other day, I never thought I'd see you outside of the hospital, but come in." He wiped his hands on his dirt-covered jeans and held the door for her.

Inside, a living room with an elevated ceiling and exposed beams lay to the right. A soft, tan leather couch sat across from a fireplace. Two striped side chairs and a walnut coffee table completed the grouping.

"Go ahead and sit down." He held up his palms. "I need to wash my hands. You caught me in the middle of my yard work."

"I heard you liked gardening on your off time. One of the day nurses who lives across the street mentioned it."

"Oh, yeah. Mildred Henderson and her family."

"I guess when you're not jogging or eating Mexican food, you spend time in your garden." Tammy smiled.

He tilted his head and gave her a crooked smile. "Yep, besides going to work and flirting with nurses on the geriatrics floor." He chuckled and strolled out of the room.

"Something I wish you'd continue to do," she whispered. Michael might never want to allow that again, and she wouldn't blame him. She glanced around the elegant living room with hardwood floors and thickly woven area rug.

Bouncing her crossed leg, she twisted the strap of her purse into coils. She tried to calm herself with a slow, deep breath. Even if Michael had changed his mind about her, he'd at least be willing to answer questions about God.

After a couple of minutes, he returned to the room and sat down adjacent to her in one of the easy chairs. "Sorry," he gestured to his messy T shirt and jeans. "I'm kind of a mess."

Under long eyelashes, his large brown eyes seemed to reflect the tension of the last couple of weeks. "Please don't worry. I apologize for just showing up."

He cleared his throat. "It's okay. How are you feeling?"

"Well. I think I'm over the morning sickness stage." She gripped her hands between her legs. "My usual strength seems to have returned."

He continued to gaze at her. "I'm glad."

"I … I'll get to the reason for the impromptu visit." Tammy rocked back and forth then stopped. Would he be willing to share the answers she needed, like she'd hoped? "A couple of days ago on my day off, I visited Big Lunas Creek in Lower Ormond Park. When Joella and I were little, our parents always told us how they used to hike the trails of Upper Ormond before they were married. Then sometimes they'd stroll along the easier paths by the creek." She smoothed the purse strap still in her hands. "The other day I felt so lonely, perhaps even empty. I thought maybe the area would make me feel closer to my parents. Maybe offer a sense of direction."

"I hope you found what you were looking for." He relaxed into the seat cushion of his chair and crossed his leg over his knee.

"In a way, yes. Though I thought being closer to Mom and Dad was the answer, I was wrong." She took a breath. "While there I had plenty of opportunity to think. For the first time in my life, I saw something about myself I didn't like. Pride. It's always gotten in the way." Tammy pulled a tissue out of her purse. "I've thought only about myself most of my life. It's been all about me, and I didn't like what I saw. As if a giant neon light blared at me in glaring colors, the word *pride* pulsated in front of me."

Michael leaned forward in the chair. "Tammy—"

"There's more. Once I came to that realization, another flagrant notion barged into my mind. I wanted to know God, the God who made the moon and the stars and humans. The God you love and serve." Tammy dabbed at the moisture forming in the corner of her eyes. "I'm hungry, Michael. Hungry for Him." A tear trailed down her cheek, and she whisked it away with the tissue. "I don't know how to know Him."

"Oh, Tammy—"

"I couldn't go to Joella." Words gushed from within now. "She'd say she could've told me that all along. I have no one else to talk to. I don't expect you to ask me back in your life after all the heartache I've caused you, but ... " Emotions flowed like water. The pregnancy making her more sensitive, she supposed. She held out her hands to him. "Just show me how to know your God."

Out the window, a ray of sun shot through the glass, casting Michael's smiling face in brilliant light. "I've prayed for you for a long time." He slid next to her on the couch. "Yes, I can help. Not because I'm a pastor or anything, but because I know what God says in His word." He picked up her hand and gently held it to his chest. "We are all flawed and sin against God. During your visit to the Lower Ormond, you became aware of the wrongs in your life, opening the door for God to work." He squeezed her hand. "Your sins are no different than mine or anyone else's. God is reaching out to you. All you have to do is say yes."

"But how?"

A joyful grin spread over Michael's face. "You can speak to Him and ask Him to forgive you for the past. I can show you how to talk to Him. Would you like that?"

Tammy batted away more tears and nodded."

*****

Michael's spirit soared as Tammy repeated every word after him. *Lord, all things are possible with You. You touched a young woman's heart and drew her unto Yourself.* "In His name we pray. Amen."

Tammy lifted misty eyes to him and gripped his hand. She sat motionless for a while staring out the window. Then she turned to him. "For the first time in my life, I feel anchored—like He has the answers to all my questions. I can't believe God would love and forgive me. I rebelled against Him for years. I wouldn't listen to anybody or any philosophy that disagreed with my summation of the way I thought things should be."

"I feel privileged to be able to pray with you."

"How can you say that? I've brought so much misery to your life."

"Yeah, but today makes it all worth it."

Her voice rose. "I never considered your feelings." She covered her face with her hands. "I'm so sorry, Michael."

He pulled her near, kissing some of the tears away. Without another word, he held her.

Tammy clung to him until her sobs subsided. Finally, she moved back and peered up at him. "In the last months, you spoke to me, not in words, but in actions. You showed incredible patience with me when I would've run away. Your unselfish attitude said so much." She reached toward his hand and covered it with hers. "You even offered to raise our baby despite the difficulties it would've caused as a single professional man. Then when you didn't give up on us after you thought I'd killed our child— " A hiccup interrupted her words. "You demonstrated true love to me. Not the kind between a husband and wife but love I would imagine God has for us." She gripped both of his hands in hers. "I love you with all my heart, Michael Clark."

Opening his mouth, Michael found no words to express the wonder in his heart.

"I don't deserve you, but if you're still willing, I want to marry you."

Again, he drew her to him. Tammy folded her arms around

him, and her warm breath on his neck soothed the tension of the last hour. How long he held her, he wasn't sure.

Later, Tammy sat back on the couch and gently patted her abdomen. "Our little baby's starting to make his presence known.

"You keep saying *he*." Michael grinned. "Is there something I don't know that you do?"

"Just a guess for now." She grasped his hand and lifted it to her lips. "Is there any way you can forgive me for what I put you through? What I almost did. I'll always regret it."

"But you didn't go through with it. God spoke to you, and you *listened* to Him. I do forgive you, Tammy, just like the Lord forgave me for my wrongs. I hope we can put this behind us and move on."

She patted her stomach again. "I'll always remember what you told me a month ago—about what God said about our child. 'Before I formed you in the womb, I knew you.'"

*****

Tammy stacked dishes in the sink of her compact kitchen and glanced over her shoulder at Michael settled on the couch. She untied her apron and hung it on the hook by the fridge. Sauntering into the living room, she sat down next to him. "A year ago I never would've predicted the turn my life has taken. But I wouldn't change a thing. I'll never regret asking the Lord into my life." She planted a kiss on his cheek. "I love you so much, Michael."

"Hey, we've got a wedding to plan." He grinned at her.

"And quick, too. I was thinking about attending Joella's place of worship. How would you feel about making that our home church and asking the pastor to marry us—if he will?"

"I'm well acquainted with Dave Reyes. Though I love my church, I think New Life would make a great place for us. Would you like me to call for an appointment?"

"Perfect."

"Oh, and another thing. Do you mind if I share with him how you asked Jesus into your life?"

"I'd be honored." Tammy cuddled close to Michael. "I realize this won't be easy. Your family may refuse to come or never accept me or our child."

"Our God is mighty, and all things are possible with Him. My mom will be in love with her new grandbaby, and Dad will come around. The Lord has softened his way of thinking. I can see changes in him daily."

Tammy played with his fingertips. "What about Darnell?"

The smile faded from Michael's face. "We can only pray for him. He's in God's hands now."

"So much is beyond our reach, like Darnell's objections to me." Tammy snuggled closer. "For years, I needed to be in complete control of my life. Now I see how much better it is when God's in charge. Especially at work. I used to feel helpless when I lost a patient. But now I understand each of us will die someday. Where we're going is the most important thing. My patients often express regret for what they'll never be able to do again. I've been at a loss to know what to say." A smile spread her lips. "Now I can share how God came into my life and the hope of the next one." She glanced at the coffee table with the Bible she and Michael had begun to read together. "Thank you for helping me to understand God's word and for forgiving me."

"When God pardons us, He doesn't remember our sins any longer. How can I not do the same?" He grasped her hand. "Look at me. I pray you can forgive me for not standing up for my convictions that night. We wouldn't be in this situation if I had."

She kissed her fingers. "And perhaps I'd never have come to believe in the Savor."

"Maybe you're right." Gripping both of her hands, he peered at her. "Would you go with me to visit Mom and Dad in a couple of days?"

Chapter Twenty-Eight

"Good afternoon, Dr. Presnell." Michael greeted the head of cardiology and newest board member in the main office.

"Please call me Don."

Michael nodded. "And call me Michael. Come on back to my office."

With a grin, Iris looked up as they walked past her desk.

"Hold my calls for a few minutes, Iris."

"Yes, Doctor." She turned back to filing papers in the metal cabinet.

"Please sit down." Michael closed his office door after Don walked in and eased into the side chair.

Sitting in the extra rolling seat, Michael peered at him. "Thank you for agreeing to serve on the board for the new hospital. I wanted to personally outline some of the plans." Michael handed him a manila folder filled with current information.

"It's my pleasure." He glanced around Michael's office. "A new hospital in El Camino is a Godsend. An answer to prayer."

Every time Michael looked at the documents that represented the new pediatrics hospital, he became more energized. After discussing the last paper in the packet, Michael sat back in his chair. "That should give you an overview."

"Exciting stuff, Clark. With God's help, you should see this completed within the year."

"I'll need to put plans on hold for a short time." Michael's insides quivered. "I'm getting married in a couple of weeks."

"Congratulations." Don stuck out his hand for a shake.

"Thank you. My future wife and I are joining the congregation at New Life Fellowship, and Pastor Dave Reyes is conducting the wedding ceremony. There are a lot of details to take care of right now."

Don's face brightened. "That's great. I'm an elder at New Life, so we'll be seeing more of each other."

Michael beamed. "Looking forward to it."

"Who's the bride? Anyone I know?"

"Could be. Her name is Tammy Crawford. She's a geriatrics nurse here at El Camino General. Her sister, Joella Neilson, and husband JD attend New Life."

"You bet. I know JD well. He serves on our financial committee." Don grinned at Michael.

A silly boy-like chuckle bubbled from Michael's throat then his smile faded. "Maybe by the time the baby arrives, the building for the new hospital will be underway."

Don cocked his brow.

"We're not keeping it a secret. Unfortunately Tammy and I got things backwards, but we love each other and our preborn child. We've both repented before the Lord and plan to disclose the truth to Dave. I suppose there's still the chance he won't marry us."

"If I know Dave at all, I can guarantee he'll agree to marry you."

"I'm grateful for your encouragement. God has been working in a mighty way in my life and Tammy's."

"Awesome."

Michael tapped the Bible sitting on his desk. "The scriptures say God works all things for good in the believer's life. That's more true to me than ever."

"I've never found God's Word to fail." Don rose from his chair. "Well, I need to get back to my office." He gripped the folder in his hand. "I'll peruse the documents again and get back with you if I have any suggestions. In the meantime, welcome to the fellowship at New Life, brother." He shook Michael's hand again.

Brother. Michael already felt a part of the congregation. "Thanks. I'll let you know when the next board meeting is."

The sounds of a booming, masculine voice filtered through the wall between his office and the outer one. Michael frowned and stepped toward the door.

Iris stood within inches of a dark-haired man, shaking her finger in his face. "You listen to me, Mister. Dr. Clark is one of the best physicians at El Camino General. I will not have you speaking like that about him. Your complaints are groundless."

Michael walked into the main office, Don by his side. "What's going on here?"

"This woman seems to be blocking my access to the high and mighty Dr. Clark." The man spewed angry words at Michael.

Michael peered at the man a moment longer, his identity dawning on Michael. "Mr. Michelfelder. What are you doing here?"

His face, scarlet, Robbie Michelfelder shouted. "I just dropped by to tell you I hope you're happy."

"Do you need help here, Dr. Clark?" Don touched Michael's arm.

"No, Don. Thanks." He turned to the disgruntled man. Memories of the day they'd lost the Michelfelder child in the NICU saddened him again. "Would you like to come into my office?"

"No, not any more. What I have to say, I can say it in front of your secretary. In fact, I wouldn't mind if the whole hospital hears." He pointed at Don who'd just left the room. "I can't imagine how you keep your job here. Negligent, incompetent, uncaring. Just a couple of the words I could call you."

"I'm sorry you feel this way, but I pride myself in giving each child the best care possible."

"Are you kidding? Look, I'm going to your supervisor and tell him what I think about you. Anything to keep other patients out of your bungling hands." Mr. Michelfelder's face turned red, and he took a long breath. "But I'm not sure what good it would do."

"What do you mean."

The grieving father scowled then ran a hand through his hair. "You professional guys all stick together. I filed a malpractice lawsuit against you after our baby died, but today my attorney said we didn't have a case. What does that stupid lawyer know? He doesn't understand the pain of losing a child." Mr. Michelfelder raised his voice. "I told him I'd find another lawyer, and he said the legal basis for this suit was nonexistent."

The man broke down, sobbing into his hands. "No one cares about our little baby. No one, and we have no recourse."

Instead of anger, compassion for the man filled Michael's heart. He knew the pain of losing a baby. For weeks, he'd feared Tammy would get an abortion. He reached out and clasped Mr. Michelfelder's shoulder, fully expecting him to jerk away. When he didn't move, Michael continued. "Sir, I understand your grief. Trust me. I've had a similar situation in my own life. The only strength I found was in God. I pray you'll allow Him to carry your burden."

The man gazed at Michael with misty eyes and nodded. He took a deep breath and turned toward the office door, shoulders slumped.

Michael paused, watching the man leave. Then he turned back to Iris. "I heard what you said about me. You stood up for me, and I can't tell you how good that makes me feel." He gave her a quick hug. "You're pretty good at setting those young guys straight and telling them off."

She seemed to study her shoes then lifted her gaze to him. "I need to tell you that I'm going to miss you very much when I retire at the beginning of June. My grandson will finish up college in the summer and has the money for his tuition saved. I want to spend some time working in my garden and taking it easy."

"I'm happy for you, Iris." Though she had caused a few bumps in the road with his project, he'd miss the dear woman. "While I'm thinking of it, I'd like to invite you to my wedding in a couple of weeks."

"I'd be happy to attend."

*****

Michael walked back into his office, staring at the floor. He closed the door and sank down into his chair, covering his face with his hands. "Lord, please bring peace to that father's heart." The inconsolable parent greatly needed God's strength to help him through the death of his child. Only the Lord could heal a person.

He pulled out his cell phone for the next task on his agenda. Making an appointment with Dave Reyes at New Life. As his finger hovered over the pastor's contact number, he chuckled. A vision of the elderly white-haired woman shaking a finger in Mr. Michelfelder's face and telling him off in her shaky voice made him smile. Finally the hardworking woman would be able to take time to enjoy the things she loved to do.

With a grin, Michael pressed Dave's direct number and waited.

"This is Dave."

"Hi, Dave, Michael Clark."

"Well, hello, Michael. I was hoping to talk to you again, to see how things were going."

"That's what I'm calling about. I'd like to make an appointment. After the last time we talked, I'd wanted to speak to you further, but things got in the way."

"Okay. What about tomorrow late afternoon?"

"Perfect. I'll be bringing Tammy Crawford with me. Just to let you know, she recently asked the Lord into her life."

"That's outstanding."

"We'd like to talk to you about marrying us." Saying the words invigorated Michael.

"Let's talk, buddy."

"See you soon." Michael ended the call and pressed the speed dial number for his parents' house. Now for the next step—to ask if he and Tammy could come by tonight with some news. He drummed a pen on the desk. The visit might prove harder than he could imagine.

WHAT GOD KNEW

Chapter Twenty-Nine

Michael rang Tammy's doorbell, feeling as apprehensive as she probably did. He tapped his toe on the hall's tiled surface. Facing his parents didn't intimidate him as much as it might Tammy. After Darnell's antagonism toward her, she probably expected the whole family would react the same, though he'd tried to assure her Mom would likely welcome Tammy. Dad? Michael still couldn't be sure. "God, please give us favor with my father and the rest of the family."

A bright smile tugged the corners of Tammy's mouth when she opened the door. A barely noticeable lump was evident under the belt of her floral dress fitted at the waist.

"You look beautiful." He stepped into her apartment then pressed his lips on her temple and counted the beats of her pulse. "Motherhood becomes you." He released her and stepped back. "I wonder who our baby is going to look like."

She laughed. "Probably like both of us."

He'd never seen her so happy. Maybe he didn't have to worry about her meeting his parents. Did her new faith in God have anything to do with the joy twinkling in her eyes?

Tammy picked up her purse on the side table and twirled around. "Is this dress appropriate? Will your folks approve?"

"I don't know how they couldn't. Come on Ms. Crawford. Let's do this." He smiled. "Oh, yeah. We've got an appointment with Dave tomorrow."

"Sounds good. I talked to Joella today, and she and Glorilyn are going to help me with speedy wedding plans. I suggested a small private service, but she insisted we have a large church ceremony." She shrugged. "Gotta listen to my sister. I'm taking a leave of absence at the hospital so I can devote my complete attention to planning and details."

"We need to talk about things, but if you want to quit work entirely, feel free. I make plenty of money for the two of us." He smiled. "I mean the three of us."

"You're sweet to offer, but I'd still like to continue with my plans to become a NP. I may think about taking an extended leave of absence until I get ready for the practical portion of the program. It would give me more time to study and take care of the baby."

He hugged her. "I'd like you to do what you feel is best."

"Shall we live in my apartment or your townhouse?" She giggled and waved her hand in the air.

"We might have more room at my place, but actually I was thinking we could build a new house. Together. You have excellent taste in decor—or we could hire your sister," he laughed.

"I'd love to live in a home we build together, complete with a nursery. Hopefully by the time the baby gets here we'd be able to move in."

Michael tapped his forehead. "My head is spinning with all the plans. Amazing how things are falling into place."

"Yes, but I still have one concern." A frown marred her beautiful face.

He grasped her hand. "What could go wrong now?"

"Your family. What if they don't give us their blessing? How could we marry in the face of their rejection of me as a daughter-in-law?"

*****

Though earlier, Tammy felt confident, assurance began to wane the closer she got to Michael's old neighborhood. Her mouth fell open. "This is the same area where Joella and I lived as girls. In fact, it was just a couple of streets over from here."

"Sure. Los Ranchos Grandes." He shook his head. "My parents bought this house when Dad retired. If I'd lived here as a kid, we might've gone to school together."

A rambling gray brick home sat at the end of the block. Michael's furrowed brow hinted he didn't feel as confident as he let on. After helping her out of the car, he grasped her hand as they walked up to the front porch past a lush lawn and neatly trimmed flower beds. Before he slipped his key in the lock, the door opened.

A charming African-American woman stood in the doorway. Her gracious smile relieved some of Tammy's nervous pangs. "Hello, you two. Please come in." The woman stood to one side.

"Hi, Mom." Michael neared her and pressed a kiss to her cheek. "I'd like you to meet Tammy. Tammy, my mother."

"Hello, dear. I can see why Michael's fallen in love with you." Mrs. Clark drew Tammy into a hug. "You're a lovely young woman."

The warmth she felt in this woman's arms stood in stark contrast to the treatment she'd received from Darnell. Tammy hugged her back. "It's nice to meet you. Michael speaks so highly of you."

The lady, dressed in a tailored blouse and black pencil skirt, smiled. "Come on into the living room. Dad's in here."

With Michael on one side and Mrs. Clark on the other, Tammy strolled down the hall. Walking into the expansive room felt daunting, yet the space gave a cozy feel with the massive fireplace, unlit on the balmy March day.

As if assuring her everything would be fine, Michael clutched her palm again. He stepped away and extended his hand toward his middle-aged father sitting in a reclining chair. "Hi, Dad. I want you to meet Tammy."

Clearing his throat, Mr. Clark, with closely cropped salt and pepper hair, stood and shook Michael's hand. Not quite a smile on his face, he didn't scowl but peered at her as if assessing the white woman his son had brought home. "Hello, Tammy."

Did the retired general approve of her? Though Mrs. Clark made her feel welcome, she hadn't been able to read Mr. Clark.

He sank back down into his easy chair near the couch.

"Please, both of you sit down." Mrs. Clark pointed to a lengthy fabric-covered couch across from the fireplace. "Can I get you some coffee or tea?"

"No, thank you, Mrs. Clark." Tammy couldn't eat or drink anything at this moment—not until her stomach calmed.

"All right, I'll check with you later." She sat in an easy chair across from her husband and glanced at Michael. "Just to let you know, I asked Darnell to come over after a while. He is after all a member of the family. I'm sorry Alexus and her bunch live so far away."

Michael scooted down next to Tammy. "You'll like Alexus and her husband and kids. Maybe they'll be home soon for a visit."

Like at the wedding. But would they hold the same opinion as Darnell, and how did Michael feel about the impending arrival of his brother? The thought of seeing him again sent shivers down her spine.

Mom glanced at Tammy. "Michael tells me you're a geriatrics nurse. I admire anyone who goes into that field." She laughed. "I'm afraid the sight of blood makes me lightheaded." Her pleasant smile once again quieted Tammy's unease.

"Ever since I was a little girl, I dreamed of becoming an RN." Tammy attempted a wide grin. "Did Michael tell you I'm continuing with my education to train as a nurse practitioner?"

Mrs. Clark nodded. "I believe he mentioned it when he called. That's quite admirable."

So far Mr. Clark sat silently observing the conversation. What was he thinking? As if in answer to her question, he finally smiled. "Well, since I don't need a baby doctor at my age, I'm sure I'll require your care one day."

Releasing the breath she'd held, she laughed and slanted a glance at Michael.

"We might as well start with the primary reason we're here." He cleared his throat. "We're open to feedback and pray you'll support us."

Mrs. Clark folded her hands in her lap. "Yes, please go ahead."

"As you know, Tammy and I have dated since before Christmas. We both realize we love each other and want to get married." He shifted on the couch. "We fully understand the issues that might come up in a mixed racial marriage, but it would make things so much better if we had your support."

"Michael knows my views," Mrs. Clark sat forward in her

chair, "but more important than racial factors are the spiritual issues."

Joy filled Tammy's heart at the opportunity to declare her new faith. "I'd like to assure both of you, I know the Lord now." She smiled and tapped Michael's arm. "Your son was instrumental in opening that door for me. Because of Michael's example, I became aware of how lacking my life was before. He prayed with me to invite the Savior into my life."

"You don't know how happy that makes me." Mrs. Clark rose and gave Tammy a hug. "Sure you two may have more challenges than other couples, but with God in your lives, you can overcome the obstacles."

Without getting up from his chair, Mr. Clark nodded. "There was a time when I didn't share your mother's faith." He glanced at Michael then to Tammy. "I understand where you're coming from, young lady. Finally one day, my wife's faithfulness in reading the Word and praying spoke to me. I recently gave my life to God."

Michael's eyes shone. "Dad, I can't tell you how that makes me feel."

"And I'd like to offer my blessings for the both of you." Mr. Clark smiled. "We support you in this marriage."

Michael stood and gripped his father's hand. "Thank you."

But would they still feel the same when they knew the rest of the story? Tammy uncrossed her legs then crossed them again. "I thank God for your support, but there's more."

Mrs. Clark's gaze dipped to the lump under Tammy's belt and up again. Did she know about the baby?

Hesitation restricted Tammy's words. "Michael and I aren't proud of our actions, but you're going to be grandparents in about six and a half months."

Mr. Clark's eyes widened. Obviously he didn't know.

No surprise dawned on Mrs. Clark's face. "I must say you two went about things in reverse. The wedding is supposed to come first, and I don't condone what happened, but I also know none of us is perfect. We all have done wrong in God's eyes." Her face brightened, and she clasped her hands together. "I'm thrilled to welcome another grandchild into our family."

"I agree with your mother. We all mess up. Me included. For too many years, I didn't live for the Lord so I know what it means to fail God." He glanced at his hands in his lap then looked up again. "I'm also looking forward to this new grandbaby."

Mrs. Clark's love seemed like that of Tammy's own mother she missed so badly. She brushed a tear away before the Clarks could see her emotion. "Thank you, both."

"Let me know if I can help in any way with wedding plans." Mrs. Clark grinned. "I especially enjoy arranging flowers. Maybe that's where Michael got his love of gardening."

Already Tammy thought of a dozen things to ask her to do. Choice of flowers for the wedding party and the church, help organizing the reception. "My sister and her sister-in-law have offered to help, but I need you as well."

"I'm ready for my first duty." Mrs. Clark gave her a thumbs-up.

Michael glanced at his father then his mother. "I can't thank you both enough for your support—"

The front door opened then slammed shut. Loud footsteps sounded from the hall. "Here you are. Am I too late for the big announcement?" Darnell scowled and plopped down in the extra side chair.

"Darnell, I thought you were coming by later," Mrs. Clark said.

He lifted two hands in the air. "Well, surprise. Here I am."

"Son, no need to be rude." She rose and kissed his cheek. "We may not all agree with each other, but we are a family, and Tammy and Michael have made their decision. We'll have a wedding in a couple of weeks."

"So you just wouldn't listen to my advice." Darnell pushed to his feet and glared at Michael. "Well, you'll find out for yourself when this woman takes you for every cent you have then up and leaves you. She'll play you for such a fool, you'll—"

"Darnell," Mrs. Clark admonished.

Michael darted up and grabbed his brother's shirt. "You need to apologize to Tammy. The woman who will soon be your sister-in-law. I won't have you talking to her like that."

"The night you came to my apartment, you never said anything like this. You claimed—" Tammy couldn't finish the sentence and say *your father was intolerant of me*. The last thing she needed to do was cause more friction in this family.

"Fine." Darnell ignored her and shook Michael's hands from his clothing. "You won't listen to me, but don't come crying to me someday when Tammy proves me right."

"Darnell!" Mr. Clark yelled.

"No, Dad. You don't understand. I never told you before. I've seen it happen—to someone I loved. She got involved with this football player, big man on campus. A white boy from a rich family who got into college with a full scholarship. She had to pay her own way and work at a part-time job. I..." He stopped and looked around, as if forgetting he was still in his parents' home. "I helped her all I could. Then she ended up pregnant. I would have done anything for her. Even marry her, but she thought the mighty football hero loved her." Darnell shook his head. "She told him, and all he could say was it couldn't be his." He kicked a side table hard. It toppled over, landing on its side in front of Tammy. "She left school. I got word, she killed herself. She took her life because she trusted a white guy who made her feel worthless."

"Darnell, I ..." Tammy started.

He raised his hand, and she stepped back. Could he really hate her so much?

Turning around, he marched down the hall, slamming the door after him.

Tears welled in Tammy's eyes, and she was now unable to disguise them. She hated bringing dissention into this family, but all along this man had been the one to hold onto prejudice. Sadness for him filled her heart. Darnell had his heart broken by circumstances beyond his control.

Mr. Clark laid a hand on her shoulder.

"Please forgive him." Mrs. Clark embraced her in another hug. "Don't allow today to bother you. My son's story and his actions grieve me. Maybe someday, he'll allow God to heal his wounds. Dad and I pray for him constantly to find the Savior in his life and rid himself of the hate that rules him." She pulled Michael into the hug. "I love you both and my new grandbaby on the way."

*****

After yesterday's uncomfortable confrontation with Darnell, Michael examined his heart. He loved his brother, and he empathized with him. Darnell had never told him about the girl in college and that shed more light on his strong feelings of prejudice against Tammy. But as long as he held onto narrow-minded bigotry, Michael could do nothing but pray for him.

He parked the Mercedes in front of New Life Fellowship. Cutting the motor, he took a glimpse at the woman beside him. Long auburn hair fell to her shoulders as she looked toward the church. "I'd give anything if my brother wasn't so opposed to our marriage. But I thank God for my parents' support."

"Another good point is Joella and her family are all for our wedding. She's just about got everything planned. Her being an interior design expert has helped a bunch."

Michael walked around the car and opened the passenger door. "Well, let's pray Dave agrees to marry us. I sure don't want to look for another church and pastor." Michael's heart pounded with his doubt.

"For years I thought I had to be in control of circumstances." Tammy took his hand and stepped out. "I think I'm finally learning that's God's job. He knows our needs and will provide the right church."

Michael chuckled. A baby Christian ministering to him. The thought warmed his heart. "You're right. Thanks for the reminder."

Like the last time he'd been there, the church office was closed. Michael pressed his hand on Tammy's back as he guided her down the same hall he remembered from the last time. A few more steps took them to an open door with the plaque on the outside, *Pastor David Reyes.*

Michael tapped. "Pastor Reyes. May we come in?"

Dave rose from his computer desk and turned to them. "Hey, Tammy. It's been a while. Come in, both of you." He smiled and pointed to a short leather couch.

"Thanks for seeing us." Michael sank down next to Tammy, and Dave sat across from them.

"I'm happy to." Dave grinned.

"Tammy and I would like to talk to you about marrying us."

Dave cocked a brow and peered at them.

"But first, you should know this amazing man I'd like to marry prayed with me to ask the Savior into my life." Tammy folded her hands in her lap. "It was through his example that I knew I needed

Jesus." She smiled at him. "My sweet sister, Joella, tried for years to make me understand, and I wouldn't listen. Finally Michael's example caught my attention. Somehow I was able to see him living out his faith right before my eyes. That and my own personal trials helped me realize I needed Someone wiser and more powerful than myself."

Dave's grin spread all the way across his face. "Praise the Lord." He slapped Michael on the back. "And now you two want to get married. I'd love to perform the ceremony, though I'd recommend you consider your home church as well."

"Tammy wasn't a church attendee before, and I think she'd feel more comfortable at New Life than at my congregation," Michael said. "We've encountered a few challenges, however. My brother Darnell is adamantly against us getting married, but we have my parents' blessings."

"Tammy, Michael, I usually ask couples to go through a six weeks premarital counseling program. How would you feel about that?" Dave peered at them.

Michael took a deep breath knowing the confession that would come next. "Uh, Dave, we'd like to marry sooner than that." He gave Tammy a quick glance. "You see... "

"What Michael is trying to say is I'm almost eight weeks pregnant."

Dave paused, staring at both of them.

"That might change everything, including your willingness to marry us. I'd understand if you say no."

Dave gave a slow grin. "The arms of our church are open to extend compassion to everyone. Christ willingly showed us grace. Shouldn't we emulate Him in our congregation? If you'd said one of you hadn't given your life to the Lord, I might have to think twice. I'm not sure if I could be party to joining a Christian to a nonbeliever." He nodded his head. "I'd be honored to marry you. If you need to shorten the waiting time, I can make an exception. I would like to ask you, however, to come in for at least two sessions."

"I'd like that." Tammy looked at Michael with a grin.

Michael let out a sigh. He praised God for His grace and mercy which he'd be lost without. "Thanks, Dave." He gripped the pastor's hand in a fierce shake. "Can we start tomorrow night with the premarital sessions?" He turned to Tammy. "If you can make it."

She nodded. "Sure."

Dave picked up his Bible off the desk. "We'll get you two prepared for marriage where Christ will be the head of your family.

Chapter Thirty

Tammy's heart soared as she glanced at her two beautiful bridesmaids in matching periwinkle blue dresses and bouquets alive with spring colors. She held her own arrangement of white roses and smoothed the long skirt of her white organdy gown. Her diamond engagement ring Michael gave her a week ago glistened in the foyer lights. "I'm still not certain I should've worn white."

"Listen, girl." Glorilyn laughed. "This is your one and only wedding. Besides you're so slender, no one can tell there's a little bump there." She gently touched Tammy's middle.

"Like mine. I'm glad I fit into this dress." Joella ran one hand over her expanding waistline. "For once, listen to your sister. You're a new creature in Christ now. God doesn't remember the past. Just enjoy your day."

Tammy hugged Glorilyn. "You mean so much to me, treating me kindly when you found out the truth then bringing Lori to talk to me." She turned to embrace her sister. "Joella, I could never ask for a sweeter, nicer sister. I love you so much. Thank you both for making this day special for me."

"I love you, too, Tammy." Joella wiped a tear from her eye. "Your new mother-in-law arranged all the flowers. She's amazing."

But what was more astonishing was Tammy's new life in Christ, her wonderful soon-to-be husband, and precious little baby. Her heart soared. God had blessed her.

JD, looking handsome in a black tux, approached from the

side hall and lifted his elbow. "Well, Tammy, Betty Ann, New Life's wedding director, is beckoning from the entry to the sanctuary. I think it's time to walk my favorite sister-in-law down the aisle."

*****

Michael couldn't wipe the silly grin from his face. Jeff Valentine and Patrick Reynolds, his groomsmen, stood next to him as Dave walked up to the podium.

The crowd filled over half the sanctuary. On the groom's side of the church, his parents sat side by side. Mom smiled at Michael, then wrapped her arm through Dad's. For a split second, a twinge of regret reminded him Darnell hadn't attended, but God was faithful. Someday He'd reach his brother.

Next to Mom and Dad, Alexus cuddled with her husband, their two children on the other side. Directly behind, a smiling Iris next to her grandson gave him a wink. Don Presnell offered a thumbs-up then smiled at his wife. Charlotte, Jerry Taylor, and a whole host of other hospital personnel sat in the rest of the rows.

As the full tones of the organ swelled, his exquisite bride floated down the aisle on JD's arm. Emerald green eyes sparkled as she arrived in the front. Michael still couldn't quit smiling when he joined his almost wife-to-be at the altar, and the two of them turned to face Dave.

As they spoke their vows to each other, Michael praised God that He had turned the ashes of their mistakes into an incredible new life together. But most important, the Lord Jesus Christ would be at the head of their marriage and home. They vowed to raise their child and any future children in the admonition of the Lord for as many days as God gave them on this earth.

"And now by the power invested in me by the state of California, I pronounce you husband and wife." A wide smile dawned on Dave's face as he glanced at Michael. "You may kiss your bride."

Tammy smiled up at him, squeezing his hand. "I love you, Michael," she whispered.

"I love you, Mrs. Clark." He supposed he'd always be enchanted by her auburn hair and sprinkling of freckles on her cheeks and over her nose.

WHAT GOD KNEW

Epilogue one year later

Michael parked a block away from the construction site on the busy downtown street. He walked around and offered a hand to Tammy in the passenger seat as she stepped out of the Mercedes.

"Thanks, honey." She grinned at him.

Baby Mike gave a little giggle.

Reaching into the back seat, Michael released the latches on the infant car seat and lifted his six-month-old son out.

"Bababa." Mike babbled his latest sound then nuzzled Michael's neck, leaving a messy drool. He'd never get tired of gazing at the round baby face, brown curly hair, almond skin, and hazel eyes more like Tammy's than his.

Tammy laughed. "I'm waiting for him to say ma, ma."

"Well, I'm not so sure what baba means. Could be Daddy."

"Ha, that's a stretch." Tammy tickled Mike under the chin and cooed at him. "Are you ready to go see Daddy's new hospital? In a few more months, it will be all finished, and we can go visit him at his new office."

Mike gave another giggle.

Exhilaration filled Michael as he grasped Tammy's hand in his spare one. Nearing the large facility that almost covered a city block, he gazed at the steel beams and the construction crane towering over the highest level. Memories of the ground breaking ceremony still thrilled him. "Only God could've put this all together—a board of directors with ten committed members, four investors, and several more interested."

"And don't forget the five well qualified doctors who are ready to sign contracts. This facility has the Lord's signature all over it."

Michael hoisted his son more firmly in his arms and smiled at Tammy. "There's still so much more to do, but the facility is becoming a reality."

"And don't forget when you resign at El Camino General in another couple of months," she lifted her chin, "I'll be able to support our family for a while with my salary as a nurse practitioner."

"I know, babe, and I thank God for your dedication to get your degree. Thanks to Mom, we have childcare, too." He kissed Tammy's cheek. "I love you, Tammy Clark."

With Tammy on one side and his precious son nestled against his chest on the other, they strolled down the sidewalk nearer the hospital. "Did I tell you? The Michelfelders stopped by the office the other day. Mr. Michelfelder wanted to ask for forgiveness for the angry scene he made when he threatened to complain to the hospital administrator about me." Michael chuckled. "And to let me know Mrs. Michelfelder was expecting."

Tammy squeezed his arm. "That sounds like good news."

"It was." If Michael lived for a thousand years, he'd never be able to thank God enough for His mighty blessings.

The End

Want to read more from this author? Books 1, 2, 3, and 4 in the Small Town Romance Series are June's most recent releases.

Letting Go

When Pastor Zackary Lawrence lost his wife and unborn child, he couldn't find the motivation to effectively pastor his church in Oak Mountain, Alabama. Now, six months later, the congregation has dwindled to less than a handful, and the bank forecloses on the building. Desperate, he takes a job at the local hardware store and reluctantly moves in with his parents.

Though Ella Russell has secretly been in love with Zack since high school, her hopes were shredded when he returned from seminary with a wife. Trying to forget the only guy she's ever loved, she throws herself into her profession as a high school counselor.

Can God resurrect Zack's life and allow him to finally discover the woman he's always loved? If Ella entrusts her heart to Zack, will he shatter her hopes once more? Book one set in Oak Mountain, AL.

Purchase link: Amazon

Prescription for Romance

Though history teacher Scott Townsend made a commitment to the Lord as a teen, he can't relinquish his bitterness toward his younger brother after he squanders their parents' money. When a beautiful, young pharmacist seeks affirmation in a way that challenges Scott's values, he must uphold his Christian upbringing. Based upon the Biblical story of the Prodigal Son, book two is set in Oak Mountain, AL

Purchase link: Amazon

A Harvest of Blessings

Nadia Maguire's son David is the only good thing that came from her marriage. After the death of her husband, she never expects to meet handsome Jared Abrams in the cemetery where she visits her dead spouse's grave. Though she falls for the handsome bank president, his daughter hurls a wedge between them. Will her life be a harvest of blessings or a season of drought? Book three is set in Oak Mountain, AL. Purchase Link: Amazon

The Long Way Home

David Maguire's tour of duty in Germany is over, and he's returning home to Oak Mountain, Alabama in search of a job. After a long flight from Frankfort, he shares an Uber with Dallas resident Jada Atwood.

Jada Atwood, a registered nurse midwife, is on her way to a medical conference in Queens. If only she could live up to her father's legacy at the hospital where she works, she could prove worthy of his reputation. Marriage awaits yet her fiancé has yet to offer a ring.

When the Uber driver must make a stop to pick up a passenger at a Queens shopping center, two men who robbed a nearby bank commandeer the Ford as a getaway car. But when they discover two passengers, they have to get rid of the extra baggage.

After the kidnappers murder the Uber driver, David and Jada fear for their lives. Will they find their way home or die in a Pennsylvania forest?   Purchase Link: Amazon

WHAT GOD KNEW

Writing a review

    If you enjoyed "What God Knew," please leave a review on Amazon. Many readers depend upon the opinions of other readers to determine whether they want to pick up a book or not. The more reviews an author has, the more likely readers will purchase the book for themselves. These days, with the abundance of talented authors, it's difficult for a writer to get his/her books out there. Reviews are the lifeblood of an author's career. They are so appreciated.

About June Foster

June Foster is an award-winning author who began her writing career in an RV roaming around the USA with her husband, Joe. She brags about visiting a location before it becomes the setting in her next contemporary romance or romantic suspense. June's characters find themselves in precarious circumstances where only God can offer redemption and ultimately freedom. Find June at junefoster.com.

If you haven't read books one and two of the Almond Street series, they are available now.

For All Eternity

JD Neilson falls in love with interior designer, Joella Crawford despite his father's command to marry a woman of his faith, the one true church, the Exalted Brethren. Yet despite his efforts to gain status in the afterlife, he can't attain the quiet peace he sees in Joella. Can he find the strength to forsake the teachings of his childhood to embrace The Truth? If he does, will Joella accept him or has he lost her forever?

Available on Amazon

Echoes From the Past

When Dave Reyes, senior pastor of New Life Fellowship discovers he has a six year old daughter, his life changes forever. He must reveal the truth to the congregation, but will they fire him and send him away in shame?

Social worker Betty Ann Johnston still grieves over the death of her police officer husband. But when he returns from the grave to torment her, she struggles to maintain her sanity. Witnessing Dave's faith is her only source of strength. Will ghosts from her past destroy her, or will she find hope in the God of the Bible?

Available on Amazon

www.ingramcontent.com/pod-product-compliance
Lightning Source LLC
LaVergne TN
LVHW012016060526
838201LV00061B/4326